2

2 0

MOOD INDIGO

MOOD INDIGO

Sally Stewart

This first world edition published in Great Britain 1999 by
SEVERN HOUSE PUBLISHERS LTD of
9–15 High Street, Sutton, Surrey SM1 1DF.
This first world edition published in the U.S.A. 1999 by
SEVERN HOUSE PUBLISHERS INC of
595 Madison Avenue, New York, N.Y. 10022.

British Library Cataloguing in Publication Data
Stewart, Sally
    Mood indigo
    I. Title
    823.9'14 [F]

    ISBN 0-7278-5452-6

All situations in this publication are fictitious and
any resemblance to living persons is purely coincidental.

Typeset by Palimpsest Book Production Ltd.,
Polmont, Stirlingshire, Scotland.
Printed and bound in Great Britain by
MPG Books Ltd, Bodmin, Cornwall.

One

The bedside alarm insistently chiming seven o'clock dragged her out of an uncomfortable half-sleep. The omens were not good: aching bones and a prickling sore throat confirmed yesterday's premonition of a cold caught from a germ-laden colleague, and the day itself looked anything but inviting. A mixture of rain and sleet hurled another pattern at the window pane, then suddenly distracted her by becoming beautiful in the light of the street lamp outside – golden arabesques drawn on black. She decided drowsily that it would make a sumptuous wallpaper and then went back to sleep until another sharp awakening sent her stumbling out of bed, already late. It was going to be that sort of a day, and if she had a particle of sense she'd stay where she was, nursing her sore throat, waiting for a better start tomorrow. But there was an urgent piece of work clamouring to be finished and no real alternative to dragging herself off to St Paul's to get it done. If there was any justice, her own germs might even find their way back like homing pigeons to the man who'd passed them on to her – the sort of colleague who prided himself on never giving way to ailments.

1

Anna brewed coffee, but felt her insides rebel at the thought of food. Half an hour later, bathed and dressed, she let herself out of the flat and squelched her way to the nearest bus-stop. She'd been barged out of her place in the queue for the third time when she was propelled forcibly from behind onto the next bus that came along. When she could turn round to thank her rescuer his friendly grin brightened up the day considerably. Chivalry was *not* quite dead, no matter what her dear but caustic Aunt Agatha always said, and feminists hadn't yet beaten the heart out of the stronger sex.

Her cold would improve, and March might just bring some signs of spring. Like many people who lived and worked in the capital, she was on very friendly terms with London's parks – knew when the willow trees would turn from black to bronze, and where the first crocuses were to be seen. Everything was late this year, discouraged by a bitter winter reluctant not to be elbowed off the scene by another season, but the spring would win; it always did in the end.

This morning, though, her thoughts clung to a different city. Where was Rupert now? Safely in New York, or still sitting tiredly in a queue of planes waiting to land at John F Kennedy? She missed him already, and he'd only been gone a day. The contentment of knowing that he was in his room on the floor below her own had been enough to keep her happy whether she saw him or not, but it had become rare nowadays for him not to climb the stairs to her studio. She knew with

2

a sharp, clear instinct that she mattered a great deal to Rupert Neville. There was pride in knowing it, and even a kind of joy, however much she reminded herself that there was nothing more to expect than this small treasure she had. She was bound to stay on the margin of his life; the centre of it was already occupied, by a wife, and by the two small daughters he would never leave. Cynthia Neville lived with them in the country, leaving Rupert to fend for himself during the week in London. She was a horse-mad attender of every point-to-point and gymkhana for miles around, and asked of her husband only that he should be on hand for weekend lunch and cocktail parties. A complacent, selfish woman, Anna thought her, from the little Rupert had let fall, but he never criticised his wife. He preferred to talk of what *could* be shared – their work at Carrington's. Only when she sometimes caught his eyes committing everything about her to memory was she uncomfortable about the evenings they spent together. He had been loyal to the letter of his marriage so far, but their situation was full of danger, and he knew it quite as well as she did. The trip to New York was providential, perhaps, giving them the breathing-space they needed.

Carrington's offices were in the shadow of St Paul's, and the big windows of her studio on the top floor spread London at her feet. Constantly fascinated by this bird's-eye view of the city, she always began the day by taking a long look at it, after running the usual gamut of moans in the big outer office – the weather, the undrinkable coffee in the vending machine and the impossible schedules set by

3

'them' downstairs were the unvarying lyrics of her colleagues' song.

The half-finished family of mice on her drawing board looked even more lifeless than when she'd abandoned them the evening before. She started on them again, and attempt number four was showing signs of promise when her desk telephone rang. The cool, crisp voice of the Chairman's secretary invited her to lay down her pencil and penetrate the holy of holies two floors below. Graphic artists – even ones as brilliantly talented as Anna was generally reckoned to be – didn't normally hobnob with the Chairman of the Board, to be promoted, disciplined, or sacked. But she was uneasily aware that Desmond Carrington was something more than the godlike figure who controlled the whole, huge enterprise. He also happened to be Rupert's father-in-law. She washed crayon off her fingers and walked downstairs, reflecting that the day was continuing as it had begun – with the ominous threat of unpleasantness to come.

She was ushered into a room that looked deceptively domestic and informal – it might have been the library of some small country house. But Anna knew it for what it was – the nerve centre of a worldwide publishing operation. She wasn't misled, either, about the man who courteously waved her to a chair. The air of a benevolent uncle lay so thinly over him that the patches of granite couldn't help but show through.

"Good morning, Miss Carteret. I've been meaning to have this conversation with you for some time, but it seemed desirable in the end to wait until my son-in-law had left for America."

Now contending with a hammering heart as well as her sore throat, she realised she'd been right in thinking that the nub of the matter was Rupert.

"I want you to resign from Carrington's," the Chairman said briefly.

His voice suddenly seemed to be reaching her in a distorted echo from far away, and she struggled to bring into focus a figure that was dissolving into a grey mist. She ducked her head for a moment and then turned towards him a face so stricken that he was startled into a truth he seemed to regret.

"Your work gives me no excuse to dismiss you; quite the contrary – it's brilliant, perhaps irreplaceable. All the same, I hope you'll agree to go."

"Why?" Anna asked baldly.

He looked irritated by her bluntness, even though it was a question she had every right to ask, but finally answered it. "I can't quite claim it as a house rule that members of the staff shouldn't get emotionally involved with one another, but such . . . entanglements . . . give rise to gossip and usually lead to grief all round."

"If you are saying that there's been gossip about Rupert and me, then it exaggerates and probably lies – as gossip often does," Anna said steadily. She could see the thin ice in front of her, brittle and dangerous, yet there seemed no option open to her but to step on it as firmly as she could.

"Are *you* saying, Miss Carteret, that the relationship between my son-in-law and you is no different from his relationship with any other woman member of the staff?"

5

A flat lie was out of the question, but she had *some* excuse, at least, for whatever evasion she could find. Rupert hadn't ever put into words what he felt about her; she only had instinct to go on, and her own reciprocating warmth.

"We're friends," she admitted at last. "Dear friends, as well as colleagues. Does that make us emotionally involved?"

"It's not quite the picture I've been given," Carrington pointed out coldly. "Your relationship is seen by others as being close and intimate."

She supposed it was as near as he could get to suggesting that she made a habit of sleeping with his son-in-law. That *could* be denied, but she felt shamed enough by the interview already, and deeply aware that she couldn't in truth claim to be talking of a mere office friendship.

"Does Rupert know about your . . . suggestion that I should leave?" she asked at last.

The delicate hesitation over the word registered and Desmond Carrington flicked his head like a horse dislodging a troublesome fly.

"We judged it better that he shouldn't know for the time being," he said quellingly. Then something in the clear gaze fastened upon him forced him to explain that 'we'. "I'm speaking as a father now, Miss Carteret, not the Chairman of Carrington's. Whatever you may say, and perhaps even believe, about your relationship with my son-in-law, I'm convinced that my daughter and her children would have a better chance of happiness if you were to leave us."

"Rupert's happiness . . . that doesn't concern you at all, Mr Carrington?"

The quiet question only hinted at the predicament of a lonely man whose daily life had almost parted company with that of his wife. This time the Chairman's eyes refused to meet Anna's and he studied an elegant paperknife on his desk as if it had materialised out of thin air.

"Rupert's happiness is bound up with my daughter's," he finally countered. "All marriages have their stresses and strains. This one has a better chance of surviving them if you are not constantly under my impressionable son-in-law's eye, making him wish he was young again, without ties and responsibilities."

Anna could see clearly now what the Carrington 'line' was to be: *she* was designated as the unscrupulous grabber of another woman's husband; Rupert was the kind-hearted weakling who had been led astray and must now be reminded that his wife and children were being threatened. Anna had no doubt of the Chairman's razor-sharp perceptions. Even making allowances for family feeling, he couldn't have missed in his daughter traits that would put any marriage under strain, and it was a sickening piece of dishonesty to ignore them so that all the blame could be loaded on Rupert's shoulders and her own. It made her want to prick the confidence she resented in him – the certainty that his famous Carrington touch could fix any difficulty.

"The stresses in your daughter's marriage haven't been *caused* by me," she pointed out. "They existed already, and my going won't change them."

The Chairman abandoned the paperknife, and his air of godlike detachment. He'd have been glad to abandon as well an interview that wasn't going quite according to plan. He had no doubt that this girl would have to be got rid of but, though she hadn't been able to deny Rupert's interest in her, it had been through honesty and not boastfulness. He watched her troubled face, wishing she looked more guilty and less ill.

"You asked me a moment ago about Rupert's happiness," he said abruptly. "I know him very well, and I think you'll destroy *him* as well as my daughter if you let him go on seeing you. I have no grounds for dismissing you, and no right to interfere in your life. If Rupert has to choose between you and his family it's just conceivable that he might choose you. But I think the cost would be too high for him in the end, and I doubt if you can truthfully disagree with me."

Anna knew what he was forcing her to look at – if not at once, then soon, the choice *would* have to be made. It would have been nice to pretend they could go on as before . . . two lonely people who were happy together; but Rupert was falling in love with her. Cynthia he might sacrifice without much pain, but not his children. Desmond Carrington was right about that. Office gossip had brought matters to a head, but the problem had been there, needing a solution for some time. It might as well be now, she realised bleakly.

"I'll go," she said, lifting her hands in a small gesture of defeat. "At once, please. I must leave it to you to explain to Rupert that I suddenly got tired of being here."

The man in front of her nodded, wishing that he didn't feel ashamed of the victory he'd just won. "Thank you, Anna. I shall keep Rupert in America a bit longer, and give everything time to settle down. You will, of course, receive a generous parting payment and, much to my regret, some other publisher will snap up the talent that Carrington's has to forgo."

The carefully timed use of the Christian name she didn't even know he knew was a last and typical touch; affability was called for now, to soften humiliation. She registered it with a merciful feeling of detachment that she knew wouldn't last very long; she must be gone before the pain started. A stumbling move in the direction of the door brought him there before her to open it. Courteous to the end, she noted; always the perfect gentleman – the Carrington touch again.

She took refuge in the nearest lavatory until a spasm of nausea had subsided, then went back to her own floor. The studio was empty and at least she could put her belongings together in peace while everyone else was still at lunch. It didn't occur to her to take any of them into her confidence; no one there had become a real friend, and no doubt the Chairman had consulted them all in the matter of her connection with Rupert. Distaste for *that* idea did penetrate her numbness, urging her to get out of the building before the usual office bush-telegraph got wind of her departure. She grimaced at the mice still sitting on her drawing board. With the usual perversity of things, they'd begun to look rather good now, just when someone else would have to finish them.

She was ready to leave when an envelope was brought in to her. Besides various official documents, it contained two things that made her mouth twist: a letter of resignation that she was required to sign, and a cheque that revealed the extent of the Chairman's relief at seeing her go. He'd been confident enough, probably, to have both letter and cheque prepared even before she went down to see him. She signed the letter and handed it back, wondering how much it had cost him in self-control not to stand over her while she did it. It would have been a fine parting shot to add the torn-up fragments of the cheque to the envelope, but she had always disliked theatrical gestures. Instead, she thrust the cheque into her handbag and shrugged herself into an overcoat that was still damp from the morning's journey in to St Paul's.

She walked away from the building in which she'd spent the last three years, and found that outside it had become cold enough for the sleet to turn to snow. Very rare for London, she decided light-headedly. One more strange event in what was becoming a very odd day indeed. There was already half-frozen slush underfoot, but the snow made a cool white curtain against her face, shutting out the rest of the world. Everything was unreal, like the darkness that descended on her a moment later as she slipped on an icy step at the Underground station and tumbled headlong downwards.

Two

Another early-morning awakening, but this time it wasn't just reluctance to get out of bed that she was conscious of. The darkness was intense, but even so she knew that she wasn't in her own bed or in her own room. Terror was a flick of fire across her body, panic only a breath away, until her eyes suddenly focused on a faint glow away to her right. A figure moved into the circle of dim light thrown by a shaded lamp and panic, at least, subsided in the knowledge that she wasn't entirely alone.

"Where am I?" she called out.

The firm, authoritative question emerged as a whisper that she could scarcely hear herself. Frustrated as well as frightened, she was about to try again when a white shape glided towards her and flicked the switch above her bed. The dim light showed her the round, kind face of a very young nurse, and the small hospital room in which she lay.

"Where am I?" she asked again. It seemed to be the most important thing to establish, though if she were suffering from some fell disease, perhaps it didn't really matter where she was.

"You're at St Martha's," said the little nurse,

smiling at her with the automatic cheerfulness that Anna supposed was the first thing the hospital's training had taught her. "You were brought in this afternoon."

'Brought in' had an ominous ring. For the moment she could remember nothing of her own accord; she was clearly in the throes of amnesia . . . but of what else besides?

"You had a bad fall," the girl explained. In case it sounded more distressing than she'd intended, she gave Anna's hand a consoling pat. "You've nothing to worry about, though – no bones broken; just concussion because you banged your head. There's a fine bruise beginning to come out."

She sounded pleased about the bruise, Anna thought with disgruntlement; but it was too much of an effort to complain – in fact, it was too much trouble to say anything more at all, and with half a sentence worked out, she abandoned the struggle and slipped back into the comforting darkness of sleep.

Sunshine was bright in the little room when she woke again; her bruised face still felt stiff and sore, but she was aware of progress. She could remember her night-time conversation with the little nurse and, by forcing her drugged mind to concentrate, she could even recall how she came to be there. There was a shadowy remembrance of men lifting her, with gentle competence, on to a stretcher, and stowing her into an ambulance. But returning recollection didn't stop there; the floodgates of memory were giving way completely now, and every grief she'd ever known, as well as the loss of Rupert and the job that had been her life for the past three years, had suddenly to be wept for. Unaccustomed tears were flowing down her face and soaking her pillow when a man's voice spoke severely beside her.

"Come now . . . this won't do."

Anna saw the flash of a white coat between her swollen eyelids. She sniffed, and glowered through her tears.

"If I feel like crying, I'll cry," she announced belligerently, but even to herself she sounded more like a sulky adolescent than an adult citizen claiming her inalienable right to do almost anything she pleased.

"There's no need to cry now," said the doctor with offensive logic. His smile was as automatically reassuring as the nurse's had been, and even more irritating. "We're going to do a scan, just to be on the safe side, but I think you're getting better."

Anna supposed that the all-prevailing attitude of cheerfulness was deliberate; if nothing else, it couldn't fail to infuriate the patients out of a harmful state of apathy. It even provoked her, very uncharacteristically, into being rude to him.

"Perhaps I don't want to get better. No one thinks to ask."

"Nonsense," said the doctor, genuinely scandalised. "You're young, and beautiful when you're not bruised and bathed in tears. If something ails you apart from a nasty tumble down a flight of stairs it's bound to look worse at the moment than it really is; but no one's unhappy for long at your age."

He was opinionated and insufferable, she thought,

13

and probably not much older than herself. But with the armour of his calling buckled on, he would slay whatever dragons of doubt or despair his patients were silly enough to confess to. She felt too tired to explain, much less argue, and simply turned her head away from him. But he saw her grimace as her sore cheek met the tear-soaked pillow, and he gently lifted her head to turn the pillow over. The kindness of it was a reproach that threatened her with tears again, but she closed her eyes tightly and, after a moment, heard him walk away.

Later that day she was trundled along to an examination room, and inserted into the strange machine that was to probe inside her head. It was a relief to get back to the bed that was already becoming a familiar refuge and slip back into the sleep her body seemed to crave. She was still drowsing when the first of the evening visitors clattered past her door into the main ward. Expecting no one, she took no notice until the brusque voice of her next of kin spoke in her ear.

"You're not asleep. I can see your eyelids flickering."

The voice was Aunt Agatha's and so, unmistakably, was the faint, fresh smell of the cologne she always wore. She put a posy of spring flowers into her niece's hands and then dragged a chair to the side of the bed. Anna buried her face in the fragrant tangle of jonquils and freesias, aware that for the moment her redoubtable aunt was less calm and confident than usual.

"I'm not as bad as I look," she insisted with a faint smile.

"You *look* awful," Mrs Prescott agreed, "but the sister I spoke to when I came in said you hadn't done yourself any real damage." She tried to sound brisk, but her hand touched Anna's in a little, revealing gesture.

"Sorry to have been a nuisance, Aunt dear," Anna said gently. "I didn't mean you to be troubled with a call; but they asked for a name to contact."

Agatha Prescott swept the apology aside. "You'll be able to go home soon, but you're to take things easily for a bit – *not* start working yourself to skin and bone again."

Anna smiled again at the succinctness of a report which was completely in keeping with her aunt's character. Mrs Prescott had never, to her knowledge, wasted anything – least of all words. Nor had she ever failed to do anything she'd undertaken, and her niece valued her accordingly. No one else in her experience had been nearly so reliable, except her own mother, Agatha's younger sister, who had died when Anna was fifteen.

"You'd better not go back to your job for a while," Agatha stated next, finally giving Anna a chance to contribute something to the conversation herself.

"I'm not going back at all. When I had the accident I'd just resigned from Carrington's."

"May I ask why?" asked Mrs Prescott incredulously. "I thought you loved being there."

"I did." Her aunt's laconic style was catching, but Anna realised that some further explanation would have to be supplied. She was hesitating over the right words when Agatha spoke again.

"Don't tell me you've suddenly forgotten how to draw?"

The question so neatly described Mrs Prescott's idea of people who drew for a living – carrying around with them a strange talent that they could easily mislay like an umbrella – that Anna grinned in spite of the memory of her last interview with Desmond Carrington. But it was there in her mind's eye, complete in every detail, down to the overpowering scent of the out-of-season lilac that had perfumed the room.

"I haven't forgotten how to draw," she answered slowly. "Dear me, no. I have it on the best authority that my work is . . . is brilliant, I seem to remember *that* was the fulsome word."

Agatha gave a sharp crack of laughter at the dryness, but waited for her niece to go on talking.

"The truth is that I was asked to resign – not because I can't draw, but because I was thought to be endangering the domestic bliss of the Chairman's only daughter."

"And were you?" Mrs Prescott queried gently.

"Perhaps, if you can call the Nevilles' travesty of a marriage domestic bliss. Rupert was lonely during the week in London by himself, and we occasionally went to a concert or the theatre together. It didn't seem to hurt Cynthia Neville, who can't tell Bach from Alban Berg, and doesn't care what Rupert does as long as he's in Gloucestershire at weekends to dance attendance on her."

"I doubt if it's an ideal arrangement from anyone's point of view, but what happened to change it?"

16

"Office gossip, mostly. I suppose people had seen us together and decided that Cynthia ought to know about her straying husband. If you've never worked in a place like Carrington's you can have no idea how people watch each other, and speculate – and even manufacture what isn't there to see. I liked to work harder than some of my colleagues, so perhaps they had an excuse for wanting to see the back of me."

"Does Rupert Neville have nothing to say in the matter?" asked Aunt Agatha abruptly.

"At the moment he doesn't even know – he's been sent off to America by our ever-tactful Chairman. But even if he didn't owe his job to his father-in-law – a good job that he does very well – Rupert would never make a fight of it. He's gentle and sensitive, not a fighting man. More importantly, there are two small daughters he adores. Cynthia Neville would probably try to destroy their affection for him if he walked out; but in any case, he wouldn't want them left solely to her upbringing."

"Leaving aside the children, it doesn't sound much of a marriage; is she content with that?"

"Content enough, I think. But the fact that he's the heir to a barony may also have something to do with it. Cynthia has a fancy to be called Lady Neville, apparently. It's the only bitter thing I've heard Rupert say about his wife."

She relapsed into a tired silence for a moment, leaving Agatha Prescott looking at what might have been the replica of a face she had dearly loved. Anna had inherited her mother's bone structure of broad brow, cheek-bones tapering to a pointed chin and the same candid grey eyes. Emma's hair had been long, while Anna wore hers cut in short curling fronds, like the petals of a chrysanthemum; otherwise mother and daughter could have been sisters themselves. Agatha thanked a merciful Lord that she could see no trace of Edward Carteret in his daughter. Even when Emma was alive it had been hard to tolerate the vain and stupid man she'd chosen as a husband. After her death, and Edward's hasty remarriage, Agatha had felt absolved from even the smallest struggle to put up with him.

It left them, she and Anna, very much alone. Mrs Prescott didn't mind this state of affairs for her own sake; her memories of a much-loved husband were comfort enough. But Anna had been left bereft by her mother's early death; she needed and deserved to be loved, not selfishly made use of by a man who seemed able to split his life in two. Agatha wasn't impressed by what she'd heard of Rupert Neville, but her niece's haunted face made it clear that he would take some getting over. Being above all a practical woman, Mrs Prescott tackled the question of the future head-on.

"Well, with no job to go back to, what will you do when you're discharged from here?"

"I'm not sure, but perhaps freelance for a bit, I think," Anna replied slowly. "I don't have to do anything at all immediately, because Carrington's paid me off with an enormous cheque by way of conscience money. But work isn't the problem . . . I'm quite sought after. The real difficulty is my poky little flat. It hasn't got a decent-sized window, and I hate working constantly in artificial light."

Aunt Agatha took a moment to think about this before her next question took Anna completely by surprise.

"What do you know about the Isles of Scilly?" she demanded suddenly.

Anna flogged her tired mind, but only two tiny facts floated to the surface.

"Early daffodils . . . somewhere off Land's End," she suggested cautiously.

"A whole group of islands and bits of uninhabited rock, thirty miles out in the Atlantic," her aunt confirmed crisply. "Peaceful except for a brief rash of summer visitors, and always beautiful. I've kept Lionel's cottage there on St Mary's, though I seldom go back now. No lack of windows because he insisted on being able to see out. What about doing your work there?"

Anna considered the strange idea. She was a Londoner, used to the pace and feverish bustle of a vast city all around her. Even if she hadn't been, an Atlantic-battered island in late winter seemed an unlikely place for the recovery of health and spirits. She was on the point of refusing it when she thought of something else: a small, remote island had this much advantage over London – Rupert would have no temptation or chance to drop in on her there. She'd made the choice for both of them and it had to *stay* made from now on.

"Thank you, Aunt," she heard herself say. "I think I'd like to try St Mary's."

Her exhausted face suggested that it was time she was left alone. Mrs Prescott planted a rare kiss on her niece's forehead and then marched out of the room, announcing that the details could be fixed later. Anna watched her go, torn between affection and doubt. Aunt Agatha's brilliant idea was already beginning to look not only ill-advised but downright impossible. Where would she find the strength to crawl out of her hospital bed, much less get herself and her possessions to an island thirty miles out in the Atlantic? The idea simply wasn't workable, and she'd have to tell Aunt Agatha so when they next met. On this discouraged note she thankfully went to sleep again, and woke to find the doctor by her side, making his late evening round. His cheerful smile still had the unfailing ability to irritate her, and his opening shot made matters worse.

"Lucky girl. I hear you're going to stay on St Mary's. It's a lovely place."

The lucky girl scowled, resenting the idea that her aunt had been discussing her with him. Undeterred, he soldiered on.

"An old friend of mine has a house there, and I usually manage to cadge a holiday at least once a year."

"Nice for you," Anna agreed coolly, and relapsed into silence again.

Simon Redfern might have been irritated in his turn except that her shuttered face induced in him a rush of the pity that doctors are expressly warned to guard against. She was like a small animal trying to protect itself against an unkind world. The wisdom of encouraging her to uproot herself and go to a strange, isolated island seemed suddenly questionable. It was certainly a desperate remedy, and he rarely set much store by shock tactics. But then he remembered Hugo. By great good fortune his friend was there, and Hugo McKay would see to it that she came to no harm.

"The islands are lovely," Redfern said again. "As soon as you're feeling stong enough, get out and really look at them. Don't just use St Mary's as a bolt-hole."

"Whatever you say, Doctor," she agreed.

The derisively obedient air brought the colour up under his fair skin, and Anna suddenly felt ashamed of herself. The man was doing his best to help her, and doctors were not allowed to tell their patients that they were ill-mannered, self-pitying brats . . . or were they? Dr Redfern was looking at her in a very considering way.

"You've been lucky to escape serious damage," he said gently. "I doubt if you've been taking proper care of yourself for some time, but that can easily be remedied. What is making you unhappy we can do nothing about . . . I wish we could."

A silence followed this little speech. Anna would have preferred to go on being irritated by him, but his face, for once without its usual smile, was grave and kind. If he pitied her, she had only herself to blame for a faithful impersonation of a Victorian maiden on the verge of a heart-broken decline.

"I'm sorry if I've been difficult . . . ungrateful for your help," she said suddenly, holding out her hand.

The gesture was much more difficult to deal with than her hostility, and the doctor blushed and stammered, "N-not at all."

The absurd little exchange made her smile, and he saw for the first time what she would look like when she was happy.

He allowed her to be discharged two days later, and soon after that, with considerable help from Aunt Agatha, she collapsed on to her berth in the night train to Penzance. She was on her way to the Fortunate Isles. Only the thought of her aunt's scorn prevented her from bursting into tears at the irony of the name. What in Heaven's name could be fortunate about a collection of windswept rocks out in the Atlantic? London had been her life; without it, she was without home, job and loving friends as well. She peered despairingly out of her sleeper window, but railway grime thwarted even a last glimpse of what she was leaving behind. There was nothing to be done except turn her face reluctantly westward.

Three

The night and the train journey seemed never-ending. With the blankets on, she was much too hot, without them not warm enough; and the narrow berth threatened either to tip her out on to the floor every time the train slowed suddenly, or to throw her against the compartment wall whenever it gathered speed. It was a relief to get up long before the train coasted into Penzance station, despite the dragging sense of tiredness that made an effort of so small a task as simply brushing her hair.

Remembering one of Aunt Agatha's many instructions, she found the luggage-forwarding office and arranged for her trunk, still sitting in the guard's van, to be shipped over on the steamer that sailed daily between Penzance and St Mary's. Feeling vaguely competent and organised, she even managed to charm a porter into carrying the rest of her luggage to the waiting line of taxis, but the driver looked doubtful when she asked to be taken to the heliport, and she saw why as soon as they left the shelter of the station yard. A wet, clammy sea-mist hung over the town, blotting out anything more than fifty yards away. Five minutes later, the heliport staff, pleasant but knowledgeably pessimistic, assured her that there was no immediate hope of a helicopter being able to take off. The forecast was bad, they added cheerfully, and if she wanted to be sure of reaching St Mary's that day, her only hope was to return to town and take the *Scillonian*, due to sail in an hour's time.

Anna climbed wearily back into the taxi which the driver hadn't bothered to move away, confident that she would reappear.

"I expect you'm wanting the quay, m'dear?" he enquired sympathetically.

She agreed that she was, wondering for the twentieth time what she was doing in this godforsaken, mist-wrapped corner of the kingdom. Had she still anywhere else to go, she would have taken the next train back to London, but her flat had been given up and all her worldly possessions were contained in the luggage at her feet and within the trunk waiting to be shipped.

The loading bustle at the quay confirmed that the steamer, at least, was prepared to take the sea mist in its nautical stride. Half an hour later she was huddled in her coat on deck, watching the grey shape of the mainland merge with the general greyness of sea and sky. The raw cold of the open air finally drove her down to the stuffy saloon below, and she sat there cocooned in misery for three interminable hours, listening to the regular hoot of the *Scillonian*'s foghorn, and trying to ignore the sickening roll and pitch of the ship as it left the lee of the mainland and plunged into the jumble of currents where Atlantic and English Channel meet in head-on collision.

"The fortunate isles, fortunate isles . . . nothing to see there for miles and miles". The words sang themselves in her tired brain with the repeated idiocy of an advertising jingle, until she was ready to weep or scream. But at last the ship's engines began to slow. She went thankfully on deck and saw a shadowy coastline gradually solidify into land. Bells clanged, orders were shouted, and the steamer slowly inched its way into St Mary's Pool and the harbour at Hugh Town, so-called 'capital' of the principal island.

Anna knew from Aunt Agatha's description that the cottage was no more than a five-minute walk away but, with a headache added to her feeling of exhaustion, she thought it might just as well have been five miles. To get herself and her luggage off the steamer looked to be only the first of a whole series of insuperable problems. The few other passengers had disappeared, and the crew were already busy loading the boxes of daffodils and narcissi which the ship would carry back to Penzance.

"Where are you wanting to go, Miss?" a soft voice suddenly enquired behind her.

The elderly purser, now free of other duties, had had time to notice her ashen face.

"It's the last cottage along the Strand," Anna stammered, "but I don't think I can quite . . ." she broke off talking to duck her forehead against the cold, wet rail. When the faintness had passed and she was able to stand up again, her luggage was already being loaded on to a hand-cart at the foot of the gangway. The purser had also commandeered its crew, and after giving Anna a quick stare the larger of the two lads suggested that they could just as easily offer her a ride too. She climbed gratefully on board, struggling not to startle her rescuers by bursting into unseemly peals of laughter. This undignified trundle through the streets of Hugh Town was a fine start to her brave new beginning on St Mary's; perhaps she should resign herself now to the idea that life would frequently insist on taking this salutary sort of nosedive into farce.

The fog had almost blown itself away during the sea crossing, and she was immediately aware of the smallness of the island she'd come to. The raucous cries of countless seagulls lining the rooftops were a background noise the islanders themselves were probably not even aware of, but she wasn't yet accustomed to them, nor to the cold, salt-laden air that scoured the grey town. Aunt Agatha's cottage was at the end of a terrace of small houses, running along one side of the road that hugged the curve of the bay, leading out of the town. On the other side of it there was nothing but a low sea-wall, a stretch of sand scarcely visible at high tide, and then the harbour basin itself, known as St Mary's Pool. The cottage was a sturdy-looking stone building, with small windows on the seaward side, a white-painted door, and a handsome brass knocker pitted by the salt air.

Anna climbed down shakily from her perch and unlocked the door. Her porters stowed the luggage inside the cottage, grinned at the size of the tip she handed them, then rattled away. The silence of the little house seemed to gather round her like a shroud and, having once come into her mind, the gruesome word refused to be dislodged. She couldn't have felt lonelier if she'd been dead, nor any colder either. Even huddled inside her coat, she was shivering like someone with a fever, and weakness made her collapse into the first chair she came to. It would have been the easiest thing in the world never to move again, and just let herself drown in the sea of frozen lassitude that was washing over her, but she was jerked out of this torpor by a sudden thud on the front door.

She went stumbling to open it and found the largest man she'd ever seen completely filling the doorway. He was shabbily dressed in corduroys and an old reefer jacket, dark hair untidy about a weathered brown face. The face itself was thin to the point of gauntness, and all his bones seemed too big for the flesh that covered them. But cadaverous as he looked, Anna had still an impression of strength, contained but irresistible; if for some reason it occurred to this giant to walk into her house, there would be nothing she could do to prevent him.

"Miss Carteret? I'm Hugo McKay. Simon Redfern is a friend of mine – he told me you'd be coming, and asked me to look in and make sure you'd arrived safely."

At any other time she would have liked his voice, deep and with a faintly discernible Highland lilt to it, but pleasure and her frozen lassitude of a moment ago were both consumed in a flash of rage. She swore silently at the interfering Dr Redfern, and then glowered at the tall figure in front of her, standing so confidently on her doorstep. Her only reason for coming to St Mary's had been to cut herself free from London and all that it contained. A fresh start, no one knowing about Rupert or the mess at Carrington's. Now it had simply followed her here because a relentless doer-of-good had labelled her as a pathetic creature who needed watching in case she put her head in the gas oven. She forced trembling legs to hold her upright by bracing herself against the wall and looked straitly at her visitor.

"I *have* arrived safely, as you see. It was unnecessary of Dr Redfern to have bothered you."

It sounded as ungracious as she'd meant it to, but she couldn't see that it made the smallest impression on the man's self-assurance. If anything, he looked amused, as might a tolerant Great Dane that allowed a Yorkshire Terrier to snap at it.

"So there's nothing I can do for you, Miss Carteret?"

"Nothing, thank you," Anna said firmly, suspecting that the conversation was becoming ridiculous; she now sounded like a suburban housewife turning a salesman away from her door.

A small twitch of the man's mouth suggested that the same thought had occurred to him, but his casual nod accepted the fact that she had no use for him. "Rebuffed, Hugo, my boy. Never mind, at least you tried," he murmured to himself. She was given a glance from a pair of dark eyes that seemed to survey her with rather weary distaste. "I'll be off, then. Good day to you," he said briefly.

He turned away and took a couple of quick strides before a soft thud made him spin round to see Anna still in the open doorway, in an unconscious heap on the floor.

She came to a moment later to find herself lying on the sofa, swaddled in blankets which her visitor must have filched from a bedroom upstairs. He reappeared from the direction of the kitchen just as she opened her eyes.

"I'm away to my own house. I'll thank you to stay where you are until I get back in twenty minutes' time."

He was gone before she could pull herself together sufficiently to tell him not to bother, and five minutes inside the promised twenty he was back, pushing open the door that he'd left on the catch. A small grey-haired woman was ushered into the room in front of him.

"This is Morag, who looks after me," McKay explained simply. "She's going to give you a hand with getting into bed."

Without more ado he picked Anna up, coat, blankets and all, and deposited her in the front bedroom upstairs. Ten minutes later she was in bed, shivers defeated by hot-water bottles at her back and toes, sipping the mug of steaming soup that Morag had brought up to her.

"I'm away now, lassie," said Morag, with the same lilting note that was recognisable in the man's voice. "I'll be back this evening to give you a bite of supper."

She disappeared with a cheerful wave, leaving Anna still swallowing her soup and wishing that the large figure lounging by the dormer window would

29

also take itself off. She was very conscious of him watching her, and surprised by the fact that Morag had gone away and left her alone with him.

"Thank you for your help, and for bringing Morag," she said stiffly. "There's no need for her to come back this evening, though."

"I know," he agreed affably. "You can manage without all this well-intentioned interference, and you'd much prefer us to go away and leave you alone."

Anna eyed him resentfully. It was exactly what she wished, but he seemed in no hurry to take himself out of the little room.

"Redfern told me he'd treated you in St Martha's," he remarked quietly. "I know he wouldn't have let you leave hospital until you were fit enough to go, but I doubt that you've been very sensible since then. When did you last have a proper meal, for instance?"

The truth was that she could scarcely remember.

"There was a lot to see to," she mumbled uncomfortably. "Then the journey didn't go according to plan because of the fog; I hadn't quite recovered from it when you arrived."

He walked over to the bed and removed the empty soup bowl from her hand, then his fingers were on her thin wrist, and Anna's quick flutter of alarm died away in the sudden awareness that he was as impersonal as a doctor . . . it was now obvious, of course, that he *was* a doctor.

"I should have explained that I'm a leech, too," he said quietly. "Not practising here . . . recuperating from a fever caught in foreign parts. But the poor local chaps are run off their feet with a flu epidemic, so I don't want to give them an unnecessary visit. It looks to me as if you just need to behave like a sensible woman from now on . . . That's to say, have regular and reasonable amounts of food, fresh air, exercise and sleep. If not, you'll do yourself lasting damage. Do I make myself clear, Miss Carteret?"

"As crystal," she agreed stiffly.

"Good! Otherwise, if you didn't look so much in need of gentle handling, I'd be tempted to beat some sense into you."

Her affronted expression brought a smile of such real amusement to his face that the artist in her was momentarily distracted by the transformation wrought in his dark, stern features. The long upper lip and straight black brows quirked upwards so irresistibly that it was difficult for anyone watching him not to smile back. She resisted the temptation, but before she could enquire whether that was how he normally addressed his patients, he'd picked up his jacket and walked to the door.

"It's a small island, so no doubt we shall see more of each other. Good day to you for the moment."

She hoped he was wrong in thinking that their paths would cross in future. His connection with Redfern almost certainly meant that he knew as much about her as the London doctor had known, and she was still painfully aware of having been far from her best in St Martha's. But apart from that drawback Hugo McKay was too large, too self-assured, too ready to believe her a fool of a woman who couldn't be trusted to look after herself properly. Anna spared a drowsy thought, in passing, for the illness that could have brought *him* to the island in need of convalescence; then, relaxed and warm at last, she fell asleep again.

Morag was as good as her word, and reappeared at six o'clock to cook a supper of scrambled eggs, toast and coffee. She sat by the bed long enough to make sure Anna ploughed through it to the last crumb and drop, and then scrutinised her patient carefully.

"Aye, I think you'll do now, without I bring the doctor back again," she decided judiciously. "There's a casserole downstairs for your dinner tomorrow, and I've put bread, milk and such-like in the larder. Shall I call again in the morning or will you be able to manage on your own?"

Her voice conveyed nothing more pressing than kindness, and a calm acceptance of the fact that people living on a small island surrounded by a great deal of water looked out for one another as a matter of course. Anna might long to be left alone, but she realised that she'd come to a little community where life was ordered differently. In Hugh Town people would insist on knowing what was going on. How, otherwise, would they know when someone needed help?

"I'm very grateful to you, Morag," she said at last, knowing that she meant it, "but I shall be able to manage from now on."

There was a slight tussle before the doctor's house-keeper would accept payment for the various groceries she'd brought, but having explained how she could be reached in case of need, she finally bustled away, promising to call in a day or two to make sure all was well. Anna promptly fell asleep again to the raucous lullaby provided by the seagulls sitting on her own roof, and when she woke next morning strength had magically returned; she was herself again. Lonely she might be, and deeply sad whenever her mind clung to the memory of Rupert Neville, but she wasn't a helpless lame duck; she could make a new life now if she had to.

With Aunt Agatha's instructions in hand, she walked round the little house, located switches and water supplies, and found herself unexpectedly pleased with what her aunt had sent her to. There'd been no chance when her uncle was alive to visit the cottage, but Anna knew that he'd been a keen amateur ornithologist when not embroiled in the mysterious higher reaches of the Civil Service. The Isles of Scilly, beautiful and peaceful though they were, mightn't have had quite such an appeal for him if they hadn't lain directly on migration routes, or been the haunt of quite so many sea-birds. As it was, he and Agatha had come often enough to the Islands to go to the trouble of converting the cottage into a comfortable second home. Spare ground at the side of the house had accommodated a new kitchen and bathroom, leaving the whole of the ground floor to be turned into one large room. One of its windows looked towards the sea and the west winds, with a view enclosed on one side by the long arm of the harbour wall and on the other by the headland which formed the slip-way for the lifeboat station. At the rear end of the room another window faced a sheltered courtyard garden, filled at the moment with tubs of dejected-looking greenery.

Anna mentally converted the sturdy dining table in front of this window into a work-table, and decided that she would take her own meals in the kitchen. The living room was a welcoming place, with a stone fireplace, comfortable armchairs and well-filled bookshelves. There were several water-colours on the whitewashed walls, signed by her uncle, and they were the work of an artist who'd been talented. She hadn't known that about him; hadn't really known him at all, she realised.

There was still tinned food in the kitchen, apart from Morag's contribution, and wine in the rack which Aunt Agatha had instructed her to use, but Anna winced at the sight of it. By the simple process of not allowing herself to think of anything but the immediate present, she had managed reasonably well so far. But an inoffensive bottle of wine was enough to undo her with a wave of loneliness. Simple meals shared with Rupert in the past over a glass of wine had held the best she knew of warmth, companionship and laughter. Those small pleasures had been not only taken away from her but smeared, in retrospect, by malice and ill-will. She turned away from the kitchen, then doggedly retraced her steps. If eating would help to stop her falling into the clutches of Dr Hugo McKay again, she would begin by eating breakfast regularly from now on.

She was upstairs unpacking suitcases when another knock sounded at the front door. It wasn't Morag, whom she'd half-expected, standing there, but a plump, rosy-faced stranger.

"Miss Carteret? I'm Alice . . . Alice Pengelly, that

is," she announced breathlessly. "I look after the cottage for Mrs Prescott. She wrote me you were coming, and I got everything ready-like. But then my husband's mother took ill and I had to go over to Penzance. I'm ever so sorry I wasn't here when you arrived . . . I hope you managed well enough."

The soft west-country voice finally stopped for lack of breath and Anna leapt into a gap which she suspected wouldn't last very long.

"Everything was fine, thank you, Mrs Pengelly. I wondered who'd been kind enough to make up the bed."

Alice hesitated a moment. "Your aunt said you'd not been well . . . I could give you a bit of a hand if you wanted me to," she suggested diffidently.

It was on the tip of Anna's tongue to refuse, but she suddenly changed her mind in case Alice depended on money earned by working at the cottage. She was also beginning to get the island message – people weren't supposed to want to be left alone.

"I'm perfectly well now, but I've got my own work to do," she admitted. "If you'd like to take care of the washing and ironing for me, I'd be very grateful."

The rosy face in front of her broke into a beaming smile. "I'll be along on Monday," Alice promised happily. She turned to go, thrusting a small package, beautifully wrapped in silver foil, into Anna's hand. "I was baking," she explained shyly. "Thought you might like a pastie for your supper."

Anna thanked her and closed the door, smiling in spite of herself. There wasn't any doubt about it – even the most determined hermit would get discouraged on St Mary's and decide he must find somewhere else to establish his solitary cell. But she was there, and for as long as she remained she must learn to live as her neighbours lived.

Four

S he was encouraged by a couple of unexpectedly
spring-like days to stroll through the small town
that straddled the narrowest part of the island. It was
like the tie of a lop-sided bow; on one side of it was
the high ground that she knew, from poring over her
uncle's maps, was called the Garrison; the larger part
of St Mary's lay on the other. Hugh Town, roughly
in the middle, seemed a settlement in miniature to
someone accustomed to the endless sprawl of London.
A strange face in late February, when visitors were
very few, was obviously worth noticing, and a second
visit to the same small supermarket was enough to
break the ice. Mrs Prescott's niece was identified and
satisfactorily placed, and Anna had the impression
that some ceremony of acceptance had been invisibly
concluded.

The mild weather also tempted her out into the
sad little garden, to prune the dead wood and push
cuttings into pockets of damp, soft earth. She had
no conscious thought about what she was doing; it
was simply memory and instinct going hand in hand.
Emma Carteret's garden had been the joy of her life,
apart from her daughter, and she'd gradually created

something which expressed her own individual idea of beauty. It had gone with the sale of the house, and Anna had never forgiven her father for uprooting them immediately Emma died. She'd been a flat-dweller ever since, deprived, like all such people, of the priceless pleasure of being able to dig her own little patch of earth and watch things grow in it.

The spring sunshine didn't last. It was soon swamped by days of driving rain and gale-force winds that hurled in indigo-coloured banks of cloud from the sea. Waves piled up against the outcrop of rocks enclosing Anna's end of the bay, and the usually placid surface, of what she now knew was called the Roadstead, beyond St Mary's Pool was a heaving mass of grey water. She lit a fire from her aunt's stack of driftwood, and then sat spellbound, watching the storm outside. It was far cry from a city where she'd scarcely been aware of the changing seasons, this monumental struggle between wind and water. She was grateful for the warmth and comfort of her firelit room, and not unconscious of the fact that the battle outside put her own recent dramas into some kind of proper perspective.

The gale finally blew itself out towards evening one day, and in the new silence Anna heard a small sound she might otherwise have missed. The whimpering noise that seemed to be coming from outside her own front door suddenly stopped; but just as she seemed to have imagined it, the faint whine began again. She opened the front door, and a small body collapsed on the mat at her feet. It was an unrecognisable breed of dog, shivering and sodden with rain, its mouth drawn back in a feeble attempt at a snarl as she cautiously bent down to it. After a moment's thought she dragged mat and dog along the hall so that she could close the front door, and then considered her visitor. Apart from his general air of bedragglement, jutting bones suggested that the creature was half-starved. She tucked an old coat round him, then heated bread and milk, added sugar and, as a reckless afterthought, a slug of Uncle Lionel's brandy. The dog lay where she'd left him, and when she offered him her nourishing concoction he was almost too weak to understand that there was food in front of him. She squatted down beside him, now allowed to stroke his wet head, reluctant to admit to herself that his condition seemed to be getting steadily worse. His body under the sodden coat felt hot, but he shivered all the time, and his breathing now came in rasping pants.

"What you need is a vet," she told him worriedly.

Something about the animal reminded her of her own sorry condition when she'd arrived on the island, and it seemed strangely important that he shouldn't have found her doorstep only to die on it. He needed help, but she must quickly discover how to get it for him. Alice Pengelly had no telephone, but Morag certainly did, and Anna felt confident that the little Scotswoman would know the answer to any question she was ever confronted with.

Unfortunately, the deep voice that answered immediately didn't belong to Morag Robertson.

"It's Anna Carteret," she explained briefly. "I'm sorry to bother you but I need a vet. Can you tell me the name of one?"

There was a small silence in which she imagined she could clearly see the expression on his face.

"I realise you don't exactly warm to my profession, Miss Carteret, but isn't this carrying prejudice too far?"

She took a deep breath and promised herself that she wouldn't reply to him in kind. "I'm not proposing to consult the vet for myself. A sick dog has just turned up on my doorstep. I don't know what to do for him, and unless I can find help he's going to die."

Her voice wobbled in spite of herself, and the doctor wasted no more time. "The vet's name is James Ferguson, but I fear you won't get him for a while. I happen to know he's over on Bryher, dealing with a sick cow."

"You mean to say that's the extent of it . . . One solitary vet! Is that all these wretched islands can muster?" she was shouting now.

"He has an assistant – usually a tower of strength, but at the moment immobilised with a poisoned foot."

She was now close to tears, ready to swallow pride, and even prudence, tactless though it might be to ask a doctor if he knew anything about the treatment of sick animals. As if her thought waves had reached him along the telephone wire, he answered the question before she'd found a tactful way of asking it.

"Perhaps two non-veterinary heads would be better than one. I'll come down," he said, and hung up without another word.

Ten minutes later he was at the door, shaking rain from his jacket. Anna led him into the kitchen, where she had now towed the dog out of the draught from the front door. The doctor knelt down and handled the animal with the large, gentle hands whose touch she remembered vividly on her own skin. It came as no surprise to her that the dog made no attempt to resent his attentions. Perhaps it was too far gone to care, but she suspected something different – a small sick dog had the simple instinct and good sense to recognise and respond to kindness.

"He's hardly more than a puppy," the doctor said. "I can give him something that will bring his temperature down; after that, it will be a question of whether food and warmth can win over neglect."

He gently prized the dog's jaws apart and dropped some pills inside. Anna had more warm milk waiting, and they watched the puppy take a tentative sip. It encouraged him enough to take another, then another, until the bowl was empty. Exhausted by this effort, he dropped his head on his paws again. Anna sat on her heels, stroking him gently, too absorbed in the dog to be aware that the doctor was studying her. A wag of the puppy's tail, faint but unmistakable, suddenly made her smile and, observing it, Hugo realised that he might have to change his first, unfavourable impression of Anna Carteret.

She looked up quickly, disconcerted to find him staring at her.

"How could he have got into such a state?"

"It's not uncommon, I'm afraid," McKay replied. "People who want to rid themselves of unwanted pets simply bring them over on the boat and abandon them

41

here. Horrendous, I know, but it's almost impossible to stop them. A lot of people bring their animals on holiday . . . come here specially because they can, in some cases."

He looked down at the puppy, now sleeping peacefully. "I think he'll make it this time. Do you want to keep him?"

"Certainly, if he belongs to no one else," Anna replied. Her mouth flickered in a wry smile. "I shall call him Ulysses – he and I have quite a lot in common."

"Ulysses . . . The homeless wanderer," commented the doctor slowly.

She regretted that she'd given too much away but, instead of pursuing the subject, he shrugged on his wet coat again, and stood considering Anna.

"You're looking better than when I saw you last . . . less lost," he said, with the unexpectedness she was beginning to get used to.

Her nod didn't encourage him to linger, and he was walking back to the front door when the drawing materials and sketch books, now neatly stacked on the work-table, caught his eye. He hesitated in front of an open folio.

"May I?" he asked, flicking over the pages. "Your work, I take it?"

Anna nodded once more, expecting the rather patronising enthusiasm with which non-artists usually met the situation, but even now the doctor didn't run true to form.

"Would I be right in thinking that you're rather good?"

42

"I'm very good," she confirmed baldly, her defences firmly in place again.

It sounded unbearably bumptious, she feared, but he would just have to misunderstand. Talking about her work would mean raking up the past – her dismissal from Carrington's, and the loss of Rupert. The wounds still bled, and she couldn't have them touched by a stranger who wouldn't know the painfulness of the ground he wandered on. Her shuttered face warned him away from further comment, and he said a quiet goodnight, puzzled to know what there had been in his appreciative remark to send her back into her shell again. Anna shut the door behind him, and remembered too late that she hadn't even thanked him for coming to the rescue again. The truth was that he had an unsettling effect that prevented her from behaving naturally with him.

Next morning Ulysses was noticeably better. His bones still jutted out of the matted, unkempt coat, but the previous night's fever seemed to have left him. He inspected the breakfast she offered – more bread and milk, fortified by the chopped-up contents of a tin of corned beef – then wolfed it gratefully. When he next signified a pressing need to investigate the garden outside, she began to feel confident that recovery was on the way.

Nibbling her own breakfast while he roamed about outside, she realised something else – anxiety about the puppy had made her forget, for the first time since coming to St Mary's, the state of her own health. She felt normal again, and there was no longer the slightest excuse to put off a return to work. One assignment in particular had to be tackled soon if she was to have any chance of meeting the publisher's deadline. She'd been offered the project while she was still at Carrington's and had turned it down, but her diffident suggestion, just before leaving London, that she could now take it on, had been leapt at. She counted herself lucky to get the job – a completely new edition of Grimms' Fairy Tales didn't come an illustrator's way every day – but for the moment her relish for it was nil. Work for a long time past had been something shared and discussed with Rupert. Now she sat, pencil in hand, conscious of nothing but the loneliness that consumed her. She needed another human being to talk to, someone to laugh with her and take her hand; missing Rupert was a physical pain that made her wrap her arms tightly about herself. He was probably back from America by now, puzzled and hurt by her sudden disappearance from the firm. The thought of what *he* would be feeling was the last straw. She sat lost in misery, tears trickling down her face, until the nudge of a cold nose against her hand made her look down at Ulysses, sitting as close to her as he could get. Another friendly nudge seemed to repeat the message that she wasn't alone after all; she had a companion seasoned by his own adversities. Anna smiled at him through her tears, dropped a grateful kiss on his head, and doggedly set to work.

The days passed slowly into spring, though there was nothing springlike about the wildness of the weather. She grew so accustomed to solitude that it became an effort to make occasional telephone calls to Aunt Agatha. Alice Pengelly's weekly visit kept her in touch with who was being born, married or even buried in Hugh Town, but Alice didn't require anyone to share the conversation. Anna said good morning to Morag, sometimes encountered in the local supermarket, but she was grateful for the fact that she never ran into the little Scots lady's employer. His image remained disturbingly vivid in her mind as it was, and she'd even found herself one morning putting on paper the interesting outline of his gaunt and reticent face.

Her only companion was Ulysses, quickly growing into a large, though still unidentifiable sort of dog. Thanks to his insatiable desire for exercise, she was getting to know St Mary's very well, but the other islands remained a mystery to her – the twin humps of Samson across the Roadstead, and Tresco just to the north-east of it were usually visible even in rough water, but Bryher tucked in behind Tresco, St Martin's well northward of St Mary's, and St Agnes away to the south-west, were hidden for the moment in a tumbled mass of white-capped waves.

Ulysses' favourite walk gradually established itself; up the hill past Star Castle and out on to the cliff top of Garrison, where rabbit holes smelt enticingly and the cushiony turf was springy underfoot. The only drawback to this southwestern tip of the island, where Atlantic waves constantly drove in and carved extraordinary shapes out of the cliffs, was that it was very exposed in rough weather. On a day even more tempestuous than usual, Anna was towed up the hill wishing that she'd persuaded Ulysses to take a more sheltered walk for once. He'd been kept on his lead in case the wind should blow him clean over the edge of the cliff, and she noticed with alarm that a small child ahead of them was throwing sticks for his own dog to chase. It was a dangerous game on such a day and she fought against the wind to catch up with him and tell him so. She was still fifty yards away when a heavy rumbling sound bore down over the roar of the gale, and the ground seemed to shudder at her feet. One moment the child was against the sky-line ahead of her; the next, he flung up his arms as he and the dog simply disappeared from view.

A horrified moment of paralysis rooted her to the spot, but she shook herself out of it to drag Ulysses to the stunted trunk of a small pine tree that bent away from the wind. With her own dog safely tied up, she edged her way to where she thought the child had been, and saw at once what had happened to him. He hadn't been blown over by the wind – a chunk of cliff had simply caved in and collapsed on to the shore below, taking child and dog with it. She lay flat on the sodden turf where the ground still seemed firm, and peered over the edge. The small white blob of the dog caught her eye first and guided her to the tumbled figure of the child, flung against a boulder half in and half out of the sea.

She went back to Ulysses and fumbled desperately in her handbag for the pencil and sketching paper she always carried with her.

FETCH HELP URGENTLY. CLIFF HAS
COLLAPSED AND CHILD HAS FALLEN OVER

She fixed this message to the notch of Ulysses' collar, tied her scarlet scarf to him as well, in the hope of making him more noticeable, and then, with her heart in her mouth, started to clamber down the cliff. She went at an oblique angle, in the hope that even if she set off a fresh avalanche of stones they wouldn't hit the child below. The cliff at that point was not a great height above the sea, but the chunks of granite were awkwardly spaced, and Anna had no way of knowing how much more of the loose scree in between the rocks had been undermined by weeks of incessant rain. One incautious move sent her sliding for several terrifying yards, but at the cost of lacerated hands and sundry bumps and bruises she was finally down, picking her way through the fresh rubble strewn along the shore.

The child, when she reached him, was alive but unconscious. The only damage she could see, apart from all the grazes on his face and legs, was one ankle already beginning to swell. She took off his shoe, wondering desperately what she should do next. Even if she could be sure there were no other injuries she couldn't begin to haul him up the cliff by herself; on the other hand, left where he was, the child was soon going to drown, because in the few moments she'd been crouched beside him the waves were creeping over the boulder that sheltered him.

She squatted down behind him, locked her arms around his chest, and began to inch herself and him laboriously back and up the tumbled scree until they were some ten yards away from the water's edge.

With a final dreadful effort she hoisted him up on to a small flat rock which still seemed firmly attached to the gashed side of the cliff. Through the rasp of her own laboured breathing, she suddenly heard a small voice say, "What are we doing here? I want to go home."

It was a whimper of extreme fear, but it made her feel a good deal better. The child was at least capable of talking, and perhaps she hadn't made matters worse by hauling him about.

"We're waiting to be rescued," she said, trying to sound cheerful. "A bit of the cliff fell down and you fell with it, so I thought I'd come and share the adventure."

The child tried to move and gave a sharp cry of pain.

"Lie still," she insisted quickly. "You've hurt your leg a bit. Can you feel any other aches and pains?"

"My head hurts, and I feel sick," he reported after a moment's consideration.

"I'm not surprised. You probably banged it on the way down." Her next question, delivered casually, cost her a good deal of self-control. "Does anyone know where you were going this afternoon?"

"Mum knows I always bring Snowy . . . *Snowy!* Where is he?" The child's voice was suddenly ragged with fear, and Anna pointed quickly to a woebegone white terrier crouching behind her.

"He's fine. You were saying . . . Mum knows?"

"She told me not to go on the cliffs this afternoon," he confessed reluctantly, "but Snowy likes it better than anywhere else."

"My dog too," Anna agreed, wondering what would
have happened if Ulysses hadn't got his own way in
the matter of their afternoon walk. They were now out
of the immediate reach of the tide, and she debated
with herself whether to stay where she was or try to
get up the cliff. The afternoon was wearing away, and
even huddled together with the dog they were getting
more and more cold and damp; but her worse worry
was that the child's damaged leg needed attention.

"Would you mind if I left you for a bit . . . Just to
hurry the search party along?" she asked gently.

The child's stricken face told her that it couldn't
be done. If no one else had been on the cliff top to
notice what happened, she would have to put her faith
in the anxiety of his parents, and in Ulysses barking
himself hoarse up above.

She sat listening to a feverish flow of talk designed,
she suspected, to make her forget her suggestion that
she should leave him, and learned from it a great
deal about Colin Grayson and his family. Dad was
a schoolteacher, but very much all right in spite of
that; Mum threw pots in a lovely, untidy barn in the
back yard. Colin was less enthusiastic about three
maidens younger than himself who often interfered
with his busy masculine life, but on the whole he supposed they weren't bad as sisters went. Anna listened
obligingly, but her real attention was concentrated
on trying to remember long-forgotten snatches of
prayer. In less than an hour it would be dark and
then their situation would be desperate indeed. Colin
finally talked himself into a restless doze, and Anna
sat holding him, wondering whether she'd been mad

to hope that someone would investigate the sight of
a dog tied up with a scarlet scarf through his collar.

The horizon-line between sea and sky was beginning to blur when the sound of voices came faintly
on the wind. She turned her stiff neck in time to see
the miraculous sight of a man crawling down the
cliff to her right. There were two of them . . . No,
a whole detachment. Within a few moments they'd
picked their way across the wave-battered rocks along
the shore and climbed up to the little platform she'd
reached with so much difficulty.

There was no mistaking the first man to reach
them; his anguished face would have told her this
was Colin's father even if an identical thatch of flaxen
hair hadn't done so. Close behind him loomed a giant
figure she had even less trouble in identifying. He
spared a quick glance at her and then bent down to
the small boy still cradled in her arms.

"He's been talking quite a lot," Anna said hoarsely.
"Apart from his leg, he only complained of a headache
and feeling sick."

McKay's hands travelled swiftly over the child,
then he looked at the fair-headed man.

"They'll have to confirm it at the hospital, Robin,
but I don't think he's done himself too much damage."

They strapped Colin to a stretcher and his father and
three other members of the posse began to manoeuvre
it carefully up the cliff. McKay watched them go and
then turned his attention to Anna, on her feet now but
hopelessly cramped from sitting for so long in one
position.

"What, I wonder, are we going to do about you?" he mused to himself gravely.

A moment later he had apparently made up his mind, and she was lifted off her feet and hitched over his shoulder.

"It will be a mite uncomfortable," he said apologetically.

"Not to say undignified," she muttered into his jacket, torn between indignation at not being consulted and relief at not having to find her own way up the cliff.

She couldn't see him smile, and only heard his solemn explanation that he needed one hand to hang on with. It was a struggle for a man who was not fully fit, and he was breathing hard by the time Anna's shoulders appeared at the top of the cliff and she was lifted on to firm ground. A moment later she was almost knocked flat again by a frenzied ball of fur – Ulysses, of course, greatly relieved to see her, and still wearing her red scarf like a flag of victory. The little cavalcade wound its way back across the grass to where an ambulance and two Land Rovers were parked, and five minutes later they were all in the forecourt of the little hospital which served St Mary's and the off islands.

Five

Anna waited for the few moments it took for Colin to be wheeled inside and then set off with Ulysses to walk back to the cottage. She'd gone a dozen yards when an infuriated roar from inside the hospital entrance stopped her in her tracks. Hugo McKay was beside her in half a dozen quick strides.

"Where do you think you're going?"

"Home," she said briefly, feeling like a child caught out in some misdemeanour.

"God Almighty, woman, have you no sense? Doesn't it occur to you that your hands have got to be seen to?"

It was only then she realised that her hands were indeed painful. A quick squint at them wasn't very reassuring – there seemed to be a lot of dried blood and dirt all caked together – but she was anxious above all to avoid going back inside a hospital.

"They'll be busy in there," she said, nodding at the hospital entrance. "I'll see to my hands when I get home."

"You'll get in my car now," he answered.

She looked up at the implacable face of a man who didn't hesitate to toss her over his shoulder when he felt inclined, and did as she was told. Ulysses followed her in, and Hugo drove them quickly through the town. He didn't stop at the cottage, but went straight past and up the hill leading to Old Town Bay on the other side of the island. They stopped outside a pleasant, rambling house overlooking the bay, and Anna was led inside to a large room at the back of the house which served as a combined kitchen and breakfast room.

"Sit down and relax," the doctor ordered, pointing to a chair at the scrubbed wooden table. "I'll be back in a moment."

Her body reacted to events at last, and she was conscious of feeling shaky and slightly sick. Her host returned with his medical bag, and took a glance at her sheet-white face.

"I'll hurt you as little as I can," he said gently.

Anna shook her head. "It's not that. I keep wondering what I'd have done if Colin's father hadn't come looking for him and spotted Ulysses. I'd been trying to make up my mind for ages whether I should stay with him or fetch help."

"Stop agonising about it. You did exactly the right thing, and my godson owes his life to you . . . Now, hang on, Anna."

Skilful as he was, the business of cleaning and dressing her hands wasn't pleasant and she got through it by concentrating hard on the absorbed face of the man in front of her. Looking up unexpectedly, he caught her out in this examination, and for a moment or two their eyes were locked in a strangely exploring glance; then, without saying anything, he went back to the task in hand. When it was done he brought her a glass of sherry, with the instruction that it was to be sipped slowly while he rang the hospital to enquire about Colin.

"Concussion and a broken ankle, but nothing worse," he reported, coming back into the room a moment later. "So now you can relax and share my supper with me. It's Morag's evening out, but this is Wednesday, so there'll be lamb stew in the oven."

"What does Wednesday have to do with it?" asked Anna, intrigued by this regulated form of catering.

Hugo's grin gleamed for a moment. "Morag is above price, but she'd be the first to tell you that her heart is not in cooking. She's mastered seven dishes which appear in strict rotation. If I happen to miss one by being out, it appears the following night and the whole programme shifts back a place."

While Anna sat and watched, he competently set the table and dished out the casserole which, predictable though it might be, at least smelt delicious. She was suddenly aware of feeling ravenously hungry, but sharpened appetite wasn't what made the next hour or so enjoyable. Companionship for the first time in many weeks would have been pleasure enough, but Hugo McKay wasn't just any companion. Anna found him intelligent, perceptive, funny and kind, and it was hard to remember why she'd been so painfully on the defensive with him until now. He talked about the islands, which he knew well, and only when coffee and brandy had been put in front of her did the conversation take a more personal turn.

"I've heard you laugh for the first time this evening.

What went so wrong that you didn't . . ." he hesitated over the next words, and Anna caught him up, regretful that she'd been labelled in London with a reputation that had followed her here.

"Didn't want to get better? I said something foolish in a moment of weakness; I'm *not* an unsuccessful suicide, about to try again."

Her spurt of anger was like a tiny summer wave frothing against a lump of Scillies granite; like the wave, it was just as unlikely to make the slightest impression.

"Simon Redfern simply told me you seemed to have been reckless with your health . . . for some reason, he assumed."

"He saw me at a bad moment, that's all. I *don't* need to be constantly checked up on. I told you that the day I arrived."

Her indignant expression prompted Hugo to a brief explanation of his own. "I once made the mistake of *not* checking, you see, and my wife did manage to commit suicide."

His voice, devoid of personal feeling, defied any comment that she could think of, and although her shocked grey eyes met his for a moment, she left him to go on talking.

"Let's go back to my question," he persisted. "You're enormously talented and, from what I know of Agatha and Lionel Prescott, had a background that was anything but deprived. Something must have happened, though, to make you so suspicious of the human race."

"The background wasn't deprived," she agreed

55

slowly. "In fact, until I was fifteen it seemed just about perfect. My mother and Aunt Agatha shared the inheritance of quite a large fortune. On the strength of it my father soon gave up being a rather unsuccessful actor, but they were happy together. Then, with no warning at all, my mother got ill and died, and the bottom dropped out of the world. She'd been such a quiet, gentle person that we hadn't realised the truth; she was the backbone of our life, and without her it simply disintegrated. My father sold the house immediately and we moved to a flat in London. I hated it, on top of the grief of losing my mother, but there was one thing to hang on to – the knowledge that I'd soon be doing what she planned for me from the moment she realised I could draw."

She stopped talking, lost in the memory of a bitterness that still had the power to shrivel her.

"Go on," Hugo insisted gently.

"My father suddenly decided to remarry. I suppose I'd have resented any stepmother so soon, but he picked a girl not much older than myself and our loathing of each other was instant and mutual. She soon persuaded him that to write off my three-year stint at the Slade would save a good deal of money, and of course it had simply never occurred to my mother to stipulate that I should inherit anything directly. My father pretended he was being generous in offering me a secretarial course instead, and had the gall to accuse me of ingratitude when I refused it. We had a monumental row and I haven't seen him or his wife since. I borrowed money from Aunt Agatha to get me to the Slade, and, when I'd finally found myself a job, spent the first couple of years paying her back. She almost disowned me over that until I convinced her that she had to let me be independent."

"So there you were, established in London, no doubt working yourself into the ground to pay off the debt to your aunt. What suddenly brought you to St Mary's."

"I became rather a lone wolf, but eventually I found a friend – someone who was lonely himself, and rather unhappy. His mostly absentee wife took exception to our friendship and her father, the Chairman of the company we both worked for, booted me out. I had a slight accident the same day, and finished up in Dr Redfern's hospital. Afterwards Aunt Agatha offered me this cottage. I'm now a freelance illustrator and, professionally at least, my departure from Carrington's was an upheaval I may live to be thankful for."

"I begin to understand why I got such an unfriendly reception that first morning . . . you'd decided to revert to being a lone wolf again – a life of work and solitary pleasures, with the rest of the human race severely excluded."

"Something like that. I'm sorry if I was rude," Anna said, back on the defensive. "But I was new to the Scillies then – still convinced that the best way to avoid personal disasters was not to get involved with people."

"True, but it's an arid philosophy. I can't believe you're not prepared to live more richly and riskily than that. I only caught a glimpse of your enchanting sketches, but it was enough to deny the idea that you take no interest in what's going on around you."

She ducked her head in a little bow for the compliment but hadn't found anything to say before a ring at the front doorbell sent Hugo out of the room to answer it. When he came back a moment later he wasn't alone: the most flawlessly beautiful woman Anna had ever seen followed him into the kitchen.

"Judith, let me introduce Anna Carteret to you. She's Mrs Prescott's artist-niece, living in her cottage at the moment. Anna, this is Judith Jackson, an old friend of mine, now also a resident of Hugh Town for the time being."

Anna sketched a little salute with one bandaged hand, thinking that if she ever needed a model to illustrate the princess in a fairy tale she need look no further than the girl in front of her. Small but beautifully proportioned, with a coronet of golden hair, and harebell-blue eyes, Judith Jackson didn't appear to have a single blemish. She threw a vague smile in Anna's direction and a glance which wasn't vague at all at the kitchen table, still littered with brandy glasses and empty coffee cups.

"We heard that there was trouble on the cliff this afternoon. Peter Hubner was talking to someone at the hospital. Were they really so desperate for help that they had to bother you, Hugo?" she queried sharply.

Anna registered two things about Judith Jackson: she wore a wedding ring, and fell slightly from grace in the matter of a speaking voice that rasped a little. Hugo ignored the air of resentment and merely smiled lazily at Mrs Jackson.

"They weren't desperate at all, but I insisted on going. It was my godson, after all, who'd managed to get himself tipped over the cliff. Thanks to Anna here, the story ended happily."

"Well, if there are any more dramatic rescues to be made, just remember you're down here to recover your own health."

A smile of melting sweetness now softened her taut mouth, and Anna admitted to herself that any normal man would have enjoyed the smile enough to miss the note of command. It was clear that these two were, as he'd said, old friends. Instead of the sense of shared companionship enjoyed a few moments ago, Anna was only aware now of being uncomfortably in the way. This fairy-like creature resented her own presence in the kitchen, and the best thing she could do was to take herself out of it as quickly as possible.

"It's time I went," she said, standing up abruptly. "Thank you for seeing to my hands, and please tell Morag the stew was delicious."

"I'll run you home," Hugo offered at once, but Anna shook her head firmly.

"There's no need, thanks. The walk home can serve as Ulysses' evening stroll. Good night, Mrs Jackson."

She hurried to the door, still clumsily buttoning her coat. It was a graceless end to a pleasant interlude, but she was sure she didn't imagine the glint of steel in Judith Jackson's beautiful blue eyes. With or without a husband, this small, formidable creature clearly regarded Hugo McKay as personal property she wasn't inclined to share with any other woman. It was a relief to leave them together and walk out into the night air.

Next morning, working with some difficulty because of the dressings on her hands, Anna was interrupted by a knock at the door. A red-haired, willowy girl she hadn't seen before stood on the step.

"Anna? I'm Harriet Grayson, Colin's mother. Robin said you disappeared so suddenly last night that he lost track of you. By the time we thought of ringing Hugo, it was too late to disturb you."

Ann beckoned her inside. "I was just about to stop for a cup of coffee. Will you join me?" She led her visitor into the kitchen, and poured coffee for them both. "How's Colin this morning?"

Harriet Grayson's blinding smile wavered suddenly on the edge of tears. "He's fine. Anna . . . we've got three gorgeous daughters, but Colin's our only son. Robin says he'd have drowned yesterday but for you. We shall never be able to thank you properly."

Anna waved away the tearful remark, and smiled herself. "I heard something about the gorgeous girls . . . a bit of a trial to their brother, I understand. Incidentally, he behaved like a Trojan yesterday; he's a great credit to you."

Harriet's expression wavered again and Anna decided that it was time to sound brisk. "We've exchanged compliments enough, don't you think? Now let's forget the whole thing!"

The visitor's own flashing grin reappeared. "Hugo

60

warned me that I wouldn't get very far with what he called effusions of gratitude!"

"I should think not indeed. I just happened to be there. You don't have to go lugging a burden of obligation around for ever more."

"Well, I'm afraid you'll have to allow us to *feel* grateful for ever more, but we'll try not to go on about it."

She wasn't nearly so beautiful as Judith Jackson; in fact, there was nothing remarkable about her at all except that enchanting grin, and a mass of auburn hair which Anna rarely subsequently saw in any state but riotously untidy. But she was immediately likable, and Anna couldn't say as much for Hugo's other friend.

"I don't suppose you've seen anything of the islands yet because the weather's been so atrocious," said Harriet, "but you must get out and about as soon as you can. All the islands are beautiful in their own way, and you'll find the people kind and very friendly."

In the face of her niceness, Anna found it difficult to say bluntly that the desire for all-togetherness was not what had brought her to St Mary's. She did her best to be tactful instead.

"I'm really here to get a lot of work done in peace and quiet – children's book illustrations at the moment, with tight deadlines to meet. Not counting the shopkeepers, the only people I know are Alice Pengelly and Morag Robertson."

"Well, you've made a good start," Harriet said warmly. "They're both the nicest of women." She thought a moment. "You've met Hugo, surely?"

"We've had a brush or two," Anna agreed, not

about to admit that, for a little while in the doctor's house, she had actually enjoyed his company.

"Hugo's my oldest friend," Harriet confided. "He looked after me like a brother when I was a struggling student in Edinburgh."

Anna hesitated and then decided to ask the question that had been much in her mind since the previous evening.

"Do you know what happened to his wife? He didn't go into any details, but he mentioned that she took her own life."

Harriet looked incredulous. "Hugo told you that? How very extraordinary. It's a subject he normally never refers to."

"Forget I asked," Anna said quickly. "I didn't mean to pry. It's just that I thought I might avoid making a gaffe in future if I knew a little more about it."

Harriet Grayson stared at her for a moment, then made up her mind. "Then I'll tell you the rest in confidence. Hugo married the daughter of a very rich man – Kirstie was beautiful, much indulged, and hopelessly neurotic. When she became pregnant by a man she hardly knew, and he predictably disappeared, she threatened to kill herself. Hugo married her in the belief that he could bring her back to normal. It even looked as if he might succeed to begin with, but he was a young houseman working impossibly long hours in an Edinburgh hospital, and so Kirstie had to be on her own quite a lot of the time. Not long before the baby was due to be born Hugo went home one night and found her dead. He'd refused to prescribe any pills for her, and he never did find out how she managed to get hold of them."

Anna nodded. "He blamed himself, I suppose? That accounts for the fact that he seems to feel personally responsible for the rest of the human race."

Harriet shook her head. "He was *born* feeling responsible, I think," she corrected Anna gently. "I don't know what Hugo felt about it because he's not a man who talks about himself, but Kirstie's father certainly didn't blame him. In fact, he finished up by leaving his fortune to Hugo, who promptly converted a derelict hotel here into a home for disturbed children. He got an old psychiatrist friend of his, Peter Hubner, over from Vienna to run it for him."

Anna digested all this information in silence, and then asked another question. "Why St Mary's? How do you all come to be here?"

"That was Hugo's doing, too. He knows the islands well because he used to spend a lot of childhood holidays here. He eventually acquired a house of his own on St Mary's, and all his friends were encouraged to come and take holidays they couldn't afford anywhere else. So we got to know the islands, too. Then we heard that a school post was vacant. Robin applied and got the job, and we scraped together enough money – with Hugo's help – to buy the house we live in on Garrison. We already had Colin and Emily, but Liza and Nell were born here. It's a lovely life; we couldn't imagine being anywhere else now."

Anna enjoyed hearing about the Graysons, but she wanted Harriet to go on talking about Hugo. "I gather the doctor's been ill," she suggested delicately.

Harriet nodded. "After Kirstie's death he threw up his Edinburgh job and went out to Africa for the 'Save the Children' organisation. He came back a month ago looking like a skeleton, almost burned up by some kind of tropical fever."

It accounted for the bronzed skin that went so strangely with his gauntness, but there was still one more thing that Anna hoped Harriet would tell her.

"Dr McKay was kind enough to clean up my hands last night, and afterwards he fed me some of Morag's lamb stew. I was still there when a girl called Judith Jackson arrived . . . I suppose you must know her, too."

An expression too fleeting to be pinned down flitted across Harriet's face. "We know her," she agreed unsmilingly. "Now *there*'s someone Hugo really does feel responsible for. Her husband was like Simon Redfern, a friend of Hugo's since their student days. He insisted on going with Hugo to Africa, but in his case the dose of fever proved fatal. Judith had been a nurse before her marriage and because she was desperate for something to do after William's death, Hugo arranged for her to come and help Peter Hubner at Fairhaven."

Anna remembered her reaction the previous evening, and felt ashamed of it. "Poor girl," she said, and meant it.

"Yes . . . I keep remembering that I'd make a poor job of life without Robin; so I can hardly blame Judith for . . . anyway, we do our best to be nice to her."

The sudden switch seemed to suggest that it took a conscious effort on Harriet's part, and Anna wondered whether an even older friend than Judith Jackson resented being edged out of Hugo's life; he seemed to have the knack of inspiring embarrassing amounts of affection among his friends. Anna acknowledged to herself that he was likeable – when not being autocratic, abrasive, or harsh – but a newcomer for whom there was certainly no room in the lists must prudently decline to get into the competition. She came to this sensible decision to find that Harriet was speaking again.

". . . You will come, Anna, won't you? Robin and the girls insist on seeing you."

It was what Anna most wanted to avoid – a time-wasting social round, or being included in the Graysons' family life because they felt indebted to her. But it was hard to say so with Harriet's eye upon her. Something Colin had talked about down on the beach came back to her and offered an excuse for a brief visit.

"I seem to remember hearing that you throw pots. I'd love to see you at work – may I come and do that one day?"

Harriet grinned at her. "It's not quite what my family have in mind, but yes, you certainly may."

She gave Anna's bandaged hand a gentle, thoughtful pat, and then went on her way.

Six

The first days of April brought Easter and a sudden change in the weather. Anna had grown so accustomed to great cloud-laden skies and a turbulent sea that it hadn't occurred to her to imagine what the islands would look like in fair weather. She'd arrived there too late to see entire fields golden with the beautiful *soleil d'or* narcissus which the *Scillonian* carried by the boatload to the mainland at the end of the winter; but now every headland was suddenly a tapestry of wild flowers instead. A sky of tender blue hung over water that shaded from emerald to indigo, and the 'Fortunate Isles' no longer seemed the misnomer of her first unhappy impression.

With calm seas, and small islands and rocks that she hadn't known were there suddenly appearing, she was enticed into voyages of exploration. It was hard to turn her back on their siren song, but she persisted in working solidly through each morning. By afternoon, though, she and Ulysses were out of doors, either wandering on foot round St Mary's itself, or going by boat to one of the outlying islands.

With the help of Alice Pengelly's weekly lecture, she'd begun to find her way round island life, and now knew that a fleet of small motor launches kept the inhabited islands in daily contact with each other. Weather permitting, they went as far as the Bishop Light, out to the south-west beyond St Agnes, to take mail, supplies and relief crews to the lighthouse. She gradually got to know the kind, sturdy men who skippered these boats, and began to understand the web of family feeling they spun for the islands' very scattered inhabitants.

As indispensable to each boat as its skipper was a dog of some kind, bestriding the foredeck with the air of being very much in charge. To begin with, Ulysses viewed sea-going expeditions with such suspicion that she decided he still associated boats with the memory of his original abandonment, but over time he came to leap on board willingly enough – determined in any case not to be left behind.

She learnt never to set out without a sketching block and a small tin of water-colour paints, despite the frustration of trying to catch effects of light and colour that changed almost as she looked at them. She also discovered the truth of what both Harriet and Hugo had told her – each island did have its own charm and its own individuality, and she always came back rearranging yet again in her mind the order in which she ranked them. Bryher finally settled down first in her affections, but St Agnes and St Martin's kept fighting it out for second place.

It was obvious that her adventure on the cliff with Colin Grayson had become common knowledge, and she suspected that Alice basked in the pleasure of working for someone who had acquired the status of a Hugh Town celebrity. She did her best to scuttle in and out of shops with the absorbed air of someone who hadn't a moment to spare, but people she didn't know insisted on stopping to say good morning to her.

She was uncomfortably aware of having done nothing to make good her promise to visit the Graysons, and was still making up her mind to call when Harriet telephoned one morning.

"You haven't come," she said accusingly.

"Sorry, Harriet – the weather's been so lovely that I've played hookey more than I should. Now I'm having to keep my nose to the grindstone in order to finish a piece of work. I will come, though."

"Come on Saturday. It's our wedding anniversary and Robin's birthday. I'm planning a grand dinner-party."

Anna hesitated, wondering how absurd it would sound to claim that she worked every evening, too. She could simply confess that she'd rather stay at home, but even that was no longer true; she was tired of her own company.

"I'll be glad to come," she heard herself say weakly.

"Dress up, Anna," Mrs Grayson commanded. "We slop around eternally in jeans and sweaters, and for once I'm determined we'll be elegant. I'll ask Hugo's friend, Peter Hubner, to pick you up just in case it should be a wet evening."

Anna inspected her wardrobe, wondering what Harriet would consider sufficiently elegant. When Saturday came she was still hesitating over a short dress of fine black wool, delicately ruffled at neck and hem, but Ulysses's approving bark seemed to settle the matter, and she was ready to leave by the time her escort's knock sounded at the door.

The smiling man who stood there was a fair, pleasantly blunt-featured stranger of forty or so.

"Good evening, Anna . . . I'm Hubner." There was a faint foreign inflection in his voice, and a strongly unEnglish grace about the way he bowed over her hand. "Harriet said I could have the pleasure of escorting you tonight, but she didn't tell me just how privileged I was going to be!"

Anna smiled involuntarily; a well-turned compliment was as good a way as any of starting an acquaintance, and it made a good beginning to an evening's pleasure. Hubner noted the smile and wondered what had brought its owner to St Mary's. The air of someone used to a more sophisticated life than the island could offer hadn't yet worn off, and she seemed incongruously out of place in her present setting.

"I'm ready, if you'd like to go at once," Anna said. "Or will you come in first and sample my aunt's sherry?"

"I came early on purpose," he confessed. "Hugo told me how charmingly this cottage had been converted. I am interested in such things, and I should love to come in and look round."

She left him to wander about while she went to fetch glasses. When she got back to the sitting-room he was at the far end, examining some sketches she'd left propped up to dry. They were a miscellany of scenes that had happened to catch her eye – an old boatman intent on steering his dinghy into harbour; an oyster-catcher admiring its own reflection in shallow water; the harbour in the misty, opalescent colours of dawn, and a skein of brilliantly-coloured mesembryanthemums flung over a grey stone wall.

"They're lovely," Hubner commented quietly. "Hugo said how good you were. These ought to be published, you know. An Island sketch-book perhaps?"

She was pleased by the compliment, suspecting that he was knowledgeable enough to make it worthwhile, but she shook her head. "Maybe when I've been here longer. I don't know the islands nearly well enough yet."

Hubner studied her work a while longer, then set down his glass regretfully. "I suppose we ought to go. It isn't that I don't love Harriet's parties, but I'm really quite content here – with such a charming and talented host."

By car it was a five-minute journey to the Graysons' house. Anna had seen it from a distance and was prepared for its superb position tucked in below the headland leading up on to the Garrison, but the Georgian elegance of the building at close quarters was an unexpected pleasure. It faced west over the sea, and a dying sunset, painting itself in crimson and purple over the darkening water, made her reluctant to go inside. She and Hubner were the last to arrive. Robin Grayson, whom Anna hadn't seen except for those few anguished moments down on the beach with Colin, came up to her immediately and dropped a shy kiss on her cheek.

"Brave as a lion, but now I can also register the fact that she's beautiful as well!"

It was becoming quite an evening for compliments, and Anna was still smiling at him when Harriet appeared – with auburn hair almost tamed for once, she was dressed in silk splashed with the colours of the sea outside her windows.

"The girls wanted to come downstairs to see you, Anna, but I just managed to impose a veto," she said. "This is supposed to be an elegant dinner-party, and, for the moment, elegance and our daughters don't go together very well. But I promised them faithfully that I'd make you come to tea on Sunday."

Anna remembered Colin's trio of sisters – Emily, Liza and Nell – and agreed that it was time she made their acquaintance.

Harriet led them across the room to a wide window-seat where a quartet of other guests stood chatting. Anna blinked at the sight of Hugo in the full magnificence of Highland evening dress, wearing the picturesque clothes without the slightest hint of self-consciousness. Odd though it was, the fall of white lace below his brown face had nothing effeminate about it. Anna's gaze moved on reluctantly to the vision by his side – Judith Jackson in a dress of hyacinth blue, as intricately folded as the drapery on a Greek statue. The remaining couple, strangers to Anna, hadn't even tried to compete with such splendour. Introduced by Harriet as Michael Harding and his sister, Elizabeth, they were slightly older than the rest of the party and not in the least concerned that his smoking-jacket was turning green with age, and her beige-coloured lace hadn't been anything but a mistake even in its prime. Judith interrupted what she was saying for long enough to throw an inviting smile in Hubner's direction and a cool nod at Anna, and then turned back to Michael Harding. Slightly nonplussed at being almost completely ignored, Anna found the beige lady's humorous eye upon her, and concluded that Miss Harding got a lot of quiet enjoyment out of watching the foibles of her fellow men and women.

Harriet's dinner was a feast, and Robin's supply of wine generous enough to loosen everybody's tongue. Sandwiched between him and Michael Harding, Anna thoroughly enjoyed herself. She found her host a simple, engaging man, grateful for a wife and family he adored, and a way of life that suited him to perfection. Michael Harding was made more interesting by the discovery that he was a writer, and therefore closely involved in a world that had been familiar to her in London. He was also a treasure-house of local knowledge, and willing to answer the questions she heaped on him. Elizabeth kept house for him, he said, as well as supervising the musical activities of Hugh Town.

"She's a fine organist," he said with pride. "If you're a churchgoer, I can promise you a treat."

Anna nodded without committing herself. The truth was that she hadn't been inside a church since her mother died. She'd made up her mind then that if her life had to change, it might as well change completely. But the decision seemed merely stupid now, and next Sunday was beginning to look like a day packed with engagements.

They were gathered round the fire drinking coffee after dinner when Hugo lobbed a bombshell into the peaceful atmosphere.

"Anna, I've been trying to persuade my friend Hubner to talk you into coming to Fairhaven, but he seems so shy about broaching the subject that it's no good waiting for him to pluck up enough courage."

The Austrian grimaced at Anna. "The Scottish bull in the china shop! I was going to creep up on you with much more finesse." The amusement died out of his face as he thought about the children who absorbed so much of his life. "Would you entertain the idea, though? We're limited in what we can offer in the way of special interests, but the children respond marvellously to anything new that really catches their attention. You don't have to be railroaded into it by my friend over there, but if you could spare the time to give them a few painting lessons . . . Don't decide now though, we can talk about it some other time."

She hesitated on the brink of refusing outright. Apart from the fact that she had more work on hand than she could comfortably manage, she was of the opinion that disturbed children were best left to people trained to handle them. But while she was still wondering how to say so tactfully, someone else answered for her.

"What a ridiculous idea, Hugo. Miss Carteret is supposed to be an artist, not a painting teacher. She can't be expected to share your enthusiasm for delinquent adolescents."

Anna registered the innuendo – she was only 'supposed' to be an artist; but otherwise the damned woman was right – she had absolutely no enthusiasm for the invitation at all. But it was unexpectedly hard to say so with the Austrian doctor's eyes fixed on her.

"I've never given a lesson in my life, to children delinquent or otherwise, and I should think I'd make a complete bosh of it. But if you really think it would help, I could just about manage one afternoon a week."

She spoke directly to Peter Hubner, but it was Hugo who answered first. "What price finesse now, Herr Doktor?" Then he turned to Anna, his voice serious again. "Judith may have misled you unintentionally, by the way. The children are disturbed, not delinquent – there's an important clinical difference. I shouldn't ask you to come if they were unteachable hooligans – they're not."

Anna nodded, becoming interested in spite of herself. She'd have liked Hugo to go on talking but Judith's steely glare seemed to be suggesting that the subject would be better discussed with Peter Hubner some other time. It also left no doubt about her proprietorial attitude towards the doctor, and, having been mauled enough in stepping on to Cynthia Neville's stamping-ground, Anna refused to repeat the experience with a woman whose spun-sugar appearance was almost certainly misleading. She prudently stayed out of the way of both Judith and Hugo for the rest of the evening, and went home as she had come, in Peter Hubner's company.

The following Sunday she wavered about going to church, but finally plumped for Matins. The sounds that Elizabeth Harding was coaxing from the organ would have been enough to snare a reluctant worshipper, but Anna discovered that there was more to enjoy than that. The Vicar conducted a simple,

74

thought-provoking service for a congregation happy to acknowledge – unlike the people she had lived among in London – that a divine hand might be concerned in their affairs. She found that she knew at least half the congregation by sight, and was surprised by a distinct feeling of pleasure at now seeming to belong in the community.

The morning's inaugural visit to church was followed by her promised call at the house on Garrison to meet the rest of the Grayson family, and the event turned out to be a riotous success. She was taken in tow immediately by the children and introduced to the entire ménage – Snowy, already known to her from Colin's escapade on the beach; sundry fat and placid rabbits; white fan-tailed doves in a decorative dove-cote, and a trio of enchanting donkeys who officially earned their keep by taking the trap down to the quay when Harriet had pottery consignments to send on the *Scillonian*.

Emily, two years younger than Colin, was a replica of Harriet, complete with flaming hair and her mother's irresistible grin. Liza, aged six, was fair and shy, and so ashamed of a temporary lisp caused by a missing front tooth that she scarcely said a word. Lastly, a ravishing four-year-old beauty called Nell made up for Liza's silence by talking without stopping to draw breath.

Tea was laid in an ugly Victorian conservatory, fortunately hidden at the back of the house. Harriet explained that they tolerated it because it enabled them to have meals in the sun-trap it provided almost the whole year round. After tea Liza disappeared, then returned a moment later with a sheet of paper and a much-chewed stump of pencil. These she shyly offered their guest.

"Uncle Hug sayth you draw like an angel, Anna. Draw me an angel, pleath."

In Anna's considered opinion, Uncle Hug said far too much, but she embarked on a picture of Liza sitting on a fluffy cloud, floating among a heavenly gang of cherubs and winged angels. Emily and Liza followed every move of Anna's pencil in a breathless silence finally broken by a howl of rage from Nell. Tears filled her enormous eyes and from the rosebud mouth poured an indignant torrent of words which only Emily out of the entire household seemed capable of understanding – there was no sign of a little cloud on which Nell, too, could float enjoyably around heaven. Anna apologised for the thoughtless omission and hastily added another cloud on which Nell, clearly recognisable from the sun-bonnet which Harriet insisted upon her wearing outdoors in the blazing Scillies sunshine, lorded it among the cherubs.

"Nuvver one, Anna," said the youngest Miss Grayson when the picture was finished.

"Next time," Anna replied with equal firmness, trying hard not to smile at the enchanting face looking up at her.

"Does next time mean next Sunday?" asked Emily, a girl who liked to know precisely where she stood.

Anna looked a question at Harriet, who smiled at her and then at the children anxiously awaiting an answer.

"Please, Anna . . . If you think you can stand a repeat performance."

"Next Sunday it is, then," the artist confirmed gravely.

She was finally allowed to leave only because of the graphic picture she drew for them of Ulysses sitting at home pining for his evening walk – and on condition that he would accompany her on future visits.

Walking with him along the beach later that evening, she thought back over a day that seemed to have marked some clear point of no return. With what she now knew of island life, the idea of coming to St Mary's to hide in hermit-like seclusion was so futile as to be laughable; but the truth was that she didn't even want to hide any more. London, Carrington's, even Rupert himself, belonged to a time she was beginning to think of with detachment; regret, as well as recollection, was losing its bitter edge.

She heard nothing more from Peter Hubner after Harriet's dinner-party, and it was a silence that she devoutly hoped would continue; then, one morning, she found him outside the supermarket, waiting for her to finish her shopping.

"If I offered to carry your basket home, perhaps you'd feel obliged to give me a cup of coffee," he suggested with a hopeful smile.

It was so near lunchtime when they got back to the cottage that she gave him bread and cheese as well, and they sat with it in the sunshine out in the courtyard garden.

"About those lessons, Anna," he said at last. "You're free to change your mind, you know."

It would have been a relief to do so. The more she thought about the idea of going to Fairhaven, the more she disliked it. Instructing others wasn't something that came naturally to her, and the truth was that only Judith Jackson's interference had led her into agreeing to it. But when she glanced at Hubner and found his earnest gaze fixed on her, refusal suddenly seemed out of the question.

"May I come for a trial run?" she suggested. "*You* must decide if you think it isn't working out. I promise not to be offended. In fact, I shall be deeply grateful!"

She had never seen anyone smile quite so completely as this man did. It wasn't the subtle transformation that she had noticed in Hugo's dark features; simply a grin that lit up Peter Hubner's entire face with warmth and kindness.

"How do the children get to Fairhaven in the first place?" Anna asked next.

"Too slowly in many cases, I'm afraid – after years of parental neglect or abuse, compounded by overworked or undercaring teachers, and impersonal authorities who can't help finding them too troublesome to fit into the normal system. It's no wonder that the children arrive here so resentful and belligerent that they sometimes give the misleading impression of being actually retarded. They *aren't* that, in fact, but they have to be eased out of a web of suspicion and despair before we can make any progress with them."

"Do you never get defeated?" Anna wanted to know.

"No. Sometimes angry at what life has done to them, sometimes discouraged by a slow response, but defeat mustn't come into it."

There was nothing boastful about the quiet reply; it was simply a matter of never giving up when a child's well-being was at stake. Peter Hubner, she decided, was a special sort of man, and Hugo had known what he was about in putting his Austrian friend in charge.

She set out for Fairhaven the following afternoon, turning a deaf ear to Ulysses' entreaty that he should be allowed to go as well. Like Hubner, she would try not to be defeated, but the truth was that she hadn't the slightest idea what she would do if the children refused to listen to her. By the time she arrived at the house she was prepared for almost anything to happen except what finally did – that she should end up rather enjoying herself.

She was led in to her 'class' like a Christian being offered to a den of particularly ravenous lions. A dozen pairs of eyes surveyed her unblinkingly, waiting for the new teacher to make a fool of herself. But the derision she seemed to see acted as the spur she needed to get started. She was hoarse with nerves to begin with, but gradually diffidence was swamped by the desire to share her own delight in painting with these unfortunate children. The subject of her first lesson had caused her a good deal of thought, but she'd finally chosen colour as the one that might have the most immediate appeal. She showed the children a painting in which no more than three colours from a standard water-colour palette had been used; then explained how all the shades in the picture had come from the mixing and intermixing of those three colours. The children progressed from looking blank, to interested, to eager, and in the end she only stopped talking because a bell clanged loudly, summoning them to tea.

Peter Hubner was waiting for her outside the room and she grinned at him with the relief of an ordeal safely over. "You don't need to tell me how it went," he said immediately. "I can tell from their faces, and yours as well!"

She agreed to return the following week, but refused his offer of a lift home, saying that she would enjoy the walk. She'd covered no more than half the distance when a car drew up just ahead of her. Hugo McKay got out and waited, holding the door open for her. The expression on his face suggested that she was to be given no choice this time in the matter of whether she walked or was driven.

"Get in, Anna," he said brusquely. "You walk as if you're tired, so don't bother to tell me that you crave exercise, or would rather crawl home than ride in my car."

She was taken aback by his roughness, but too puzzled by it to feel offended. "I don't have any objection to a lift," she commented mildly, "but I refused Peter's offer, and I had no idea that *you* were working today."

"I asked Judith to tell you that I'd dropped by, and would be ready to leave in ten minutes. She must have just missed you, I suppose."

Anna said nothing, unwilling to point out that she'd

passed the woman in the grounds of the house. They'd exchanged minimal smiles, but no conversation, and the deliberate suppression of his message only confirmed what Anna already knew – that she'd been warned off Judith's personal property. It was scarcely a reflection to be shared with the man himself; nor could she explain why it seemed prudent to make a point of avoiding him in future. It would be sad if he assumed from that that she disliked him, but even small-island life wasn't without its traps for the unwary. Deep in thought, she didn't realise that Hugo had also misinterpreted the silence in the car.

"Did I shout at you a moment ago?" he enquired gravely at last.

"You didn't actually raise your voice," she said with a touch of coolness; but she made the mistake of looking at him, and saw the smile that lifted the corner of his long mouth. When he turned towards her she had the heady sensation that the car had suddenly become airborne, but he hauled them back to safe ground with another, rather breathless question.

"How did the lesson go?"

"Very badly to begin with, because the teacher was nearly inaudible with nerves, but I think it finished up all right . . . Well enough, anyway, for Peter to want me to go back next week."

Hugo started to say something, but changed his mind, and for the rest of the short journey they said nothing at all. The easy companionship of their supper after the cliff rescue had deserted them now. Instead, tension crackled across the too-small gap that separated them in the car. She knew that they were both aware of it, and suspected him of making the same resolution as herself: their visiting days at Fairhaven had much better not coincide in future. She didn't like Judith Jackson, but the woman had tragically lost a husband, and must be forgiven for staking her claim to a replacement happiness. Anna shied away from any sort of claim for herself, refusing to accept Hugo in the quiet places of her mind where she'd been accustomed to look for Rupert. It was becoming an effort even to recollect Rupert's face; but there was no difficulty in estimating the lunacy of finding Judith's choice indispensable to her own happiness – that way madness truly would lie.

She got out of the car at the cottage door almost before it stopped, smiled briefly at him by way of goodbye, and bolted indoors. It was pitifully adolescent behaviour, she conceded afterwards to Ulysses; but one way and another the whole afternoon had been a severe strain.

Seven

It was becoming hard to complete the Grimms' Fairy Tales illustrations on time. A peaceful, lonely life dedicated to work and whatever recuperation the islands offered now seemed laughably far removed from the web of relationships being woven around her. Ulysses, much more companion than pet, absorbed more of each day than any other mere dog would have done, but the demands of friends were becoming insistent, too. Her weekly visits to the Graysons and to Fairhaven had become an established routine, and there were frequent evenings spent with the Hardings, Peter Hubner, and the other people to whom they were intent on introducing her. It was useless to protest – living on a small island meant, they said, taking an interest in the people she shared that island with. So, with her dream of a quiet life already in tatters, Anna did no more than groan when she put the receiver down one morning after a telephone conversation with her aunt. Agatha Prescott proposed to pay St Mary's a visit, and had announced her intention as usual with the minimum of words and advance notice.

With Alice's enthusiastic help, the cottage was scoured and polished, and bedecked with flowers; the larder was stocked, and the inroads in the wine-rack made good. Then, with Ulysses brushed to a state of rare and unnatural neatness, Anna presented herself at the quay to await the arrival of the *Scillonian* – her aunt still predictably refusing to admit that the helicopter had been invented. Watching the unmistakable figure march briskly down the gangway, Anna was suddenly overcome with pleasure and surprised them both by enveloping the new arrival in a warm hug. Agatha surveyed her niece's tanned, smiling face with an expression of grim approval.

"You look better," she announced accusingly. Unused to such gruffness, Ulysses uttered a warning bark, and she observed him for the first time. "What in the name of heaven is that?"

Anna's grin acknowledged that the question was justified. Now that he was almost fully grown, her dog's mixed parentage was becoming very noticeable.

"This is my friend, Ulysses," she said proudly. "Our paths crossed accidentally soon after I got here. He's a rare mixture – retriever and setter, wouldn't you say, with perhaps a dash of bassett hound as well?"

Aunt Agatha and Ulysses took another look at one another, and agreed that first impressions might have been mutually misleading.

Anna took her aunt's small suitcase and the three of them walked back along the quay and through the town. The stroll turned into something of a royal progress, with Aunt Agatha bowing to left and right at everyone who recognised her. Anna rejoiced in the perfect morning, taking a proprietary pride in the fact that St Mary's was looking its very best. Brilliant sunshine lay over the island, but there was a stiff breeze to temper the heat and fleck the dark-blue sea with white. Hugh Town was beginning to fill with summer visitors, but not so unpleasantly that it had become crowded or raucous; it was simply a small town humming with life and the special air of gaiety that comes with pleasant people enjoying themselves on holiday.

While Anna got lunch, Aunt Agatha allowed herself to be settled in the sunshine in the garden, with a glass of sherry on the table by her side, and Ulysses sitting nearby to keep a companionable eye on her. Mrs Prescott was aware of feeling unusually benign. Anna still looked slender but no longer painfully thin, and it was obvious that she was well again. The work spread out on her table indicated that she was busy, and the cottage itself spoke of the loving care that was being lavished upon it. In fact, her niece seemed to have advanced so far along the road towards serenity that Agatha Prescott was reluctant to broach the real reason for her visit. She hesitated in a way that was foreign to her forthright nature, avoiding the subject until they were beside the sitting-room fire Anna had lit as the evening turned cool.

"I had a visit from Rupert Neville the other day," she announced abruptly. "He wanted to know where you were."

Anna put down her coffee cup with extreme care. "Did you tell him?" she enquired after a pause.

"No. I couldn't do that without your permission. But I did promise to let you know he'd been to see me. I said it was up to you to contact him if you wanted to." She waited a moment, watching her niece's face. "Shall you . . . get in touch with him?" she asked gently.

Anna stared at the flames curling round the driftwood in the grate, taking time to answer. "No, I don't think so. I promised Desmond Carrington that I wouldn't encourage Rupert to see me. Even if I hadn't, I can't imagine that anything has changed . . . so where would be the point?"

The words were true, but they were not the whole truth. There might not have been any change in Rupert, but she was now conscious of a world of difference in herself. "I'm content here," she went on more firmly. "So content, in fact, that I'd be happy to stay until such time as you want the cottage back."

Aunt Agatha shook her head. "I don't want it back at all. If you like it here, the cottage becomes yours. I came prepared and hoping for that." She opened her large, old-fashioned handbag and rummaged inside for a bundle of papers. "Title deeds," she explained briefly. "I hoped you'd fall in love with the place and not want to rush back to London. That doesn't mean you have to spend the rest of your life here, but if the cottage is yours I can be sure you'll always have a home to come to."

Anna struggled to overcome the tears that her aunt would certainly despise, and went over to deposit a kiss on her cheek instead. "Dear aunt, what a gift! Thank you more than I can possibly say. I shall cherish it more than ever, and badger you to come and stay with me in and out of season."

Over breakfast next morning she explained the itinerary for the day. Morning service was no surprise to Mrs Prescott – she belonged to a generation that saw nothing odd in going to church; but chance had never before thrown the Graysons in her way. The family having made frequent, graphic appearances in her niece's letters, she raised no objection to being included in the usual Sunday afternoon visit, and Anna herself waited with interest to see what Aunt Agatha and the youngest Miss Grayson would make of each other – she judged them evenly matched opponents in the game of hogging most of everyone else's attention.

First, though, it was Holy Communion at half-past ten. Anna resigned herself to the fact that her usual pew at the back of the church wouldn't do for her aunt, who had an ineradicable belief that her natural place lay at the centre of things. After the service there were so many people to be greeted that by the time they'd reached the churchyard outside it was no surprise to see most of the congregation already there, chatting and slowly making its way home. Hugo, towering head and shoulders above everyone else, could hardly be missed, but he seemed to be deep in conversation with the vet. With any luck, Anna reckoned, there would be no need to . . . but the thought, not even completed, was slaughtered by a commanding wave from her aunt that would have done credit to a great actress playing Lady Bracknell. The doctor excused himself from James Ferguson and came over at once to bend low enough to plant a kiss on Mrs Prescott's cheek. A measuring glance at Anna seemed to suggest that he thought of giving her the same treatment, but she scowled so ferociously that he straightened up and offered her a very formal bow instead.

"Hugo, I'm glad to see you," Agatha announced briskly. "Have you taken my advice yet and found yourself a wife?"

Anna winced inwardly at this piece of gratuitous and probably painful interference but it appeared to give no offence.

"Not quite," he admitted calmly, "but I'm working on it." He looked at the silent Anna, her dark head as lustrous as a blackbird's wing in the sunlight. "We're making a good job of *her*, don't you think?" he asked Mrs Prescott.

There was no chance to retaliate. Peter Hubner, having completed his sidesman's duties, had come out of the church to join them. Hugo introduced him to Agatha and the Austrian bowed over her hand with his usual charming grace.

"I'm delighted to meet you," he said gravely. "I believe you were instrumental in sending Anna to us."

The warmth of his glance was not lost on Aunt Agatha, and she looked consideringly from one to the other of the two men: the stocky, gentle Austrian, and Hugo towering by his side, dark hair ruffled by the breeze as usual.

"My niece was supposed to be coming here for a quiet life. I begin to wonder how she gets any work done," she observed with the trenchancy Hugo was accustomed to but the startled Hubner was not.

The four of them set off down towards the strand,

Peter and Anna falling into step behind the other two, content not to catch them up. By the time they reached the cottage it was a relief to see that Hugo had already escorted Mrs Prescott to the door and said goodbye. She looked thoughtful over lunch but baulked at asking outright about the men who now seemed to clutter up her niece's life. Anna felt no obligation to enlighten her.

Afternoon tea with the Graysons was all she could have hoped and more. Emily and Robin considerately arrived in the trap, with two of the donkeys harnessed to it, to spare an elderly visitor the climb up to the Garrison. Then Robin and Anna strolled behind, and Aunt Agatha, looking very much like the late Queen Mary, was installed inside while Emily importantly took charge.

With this unfair head-start on the part of her eldest sister, and with Colin made interesting by a leg still in plaster, Nell had to exert herself to make her usual impression on the newcomer. She achieved it accidentally at the price of a spectacular tumble from the top of the garden steps and, as usual, this outrage to her person made her angry rather than tearful. She surveyed a pair of badly grazed knees, but the scream of rage she was about to unleash never materialised.

"You're going to be very brave and not make any fuss at all, aren't you?" said Aunt Agatha with a certainty not to be denied.

Nell exchanged a long stare with this formidable lady and finally made up her mind. "Yes," she agreed with a blinding smile.

She allowed her grazes to be cleaned and dressed,

then signified that she wished, in this wounded state, to remain on no one's knee but Aunt Agatha's. Redoubtable though she was, even Mrs Prescott wasn't immune to this kind of flattery. Exchanging grins with Harriet, Anna decided that life in recent weeks had become astonishingly enjoyable.

Two days later her aunt was conducted back to the steamer, and Anna found that she missed her relative's astringent company. On her own again, she also had to consider what to do about the fact that Rupert had been trying to get in touch with her. She knew enough about Cynthia Neville to be certain that an amicable divorce was not in question, even if Rupert himself had reached the unlikely point of deciding to cut himself off from the small daughters he adored. The only possible explanation of his efforts to get in touch was that, now back in London himself, he felt concerned about her – perhaps aware of the reason for her departure, and feeling largely responsible.

She wasted a lot of midnight oil starting letters that found their way eventually into the waste-paper basket, either because they sounded hurtfully formal or were liable to be misunderstood. At last she arrived at a compromise that would have to do. Not knowing how much of her interview with Desmond Carrington had been relayed to Rupert, she simply said that it had been judged best for her to leave the company. She thanked him for much kindness and happiness in the past, stressed that she was well and very busy, and confirmed that she had no thought of returning to London. Her address was omitted deliberately, and she hoped this would make it clear to Rupert that she was not looking for a letter in return. He belonged to a part of her life that was over, and she saw this clearly enough now to understand that Desmond Carrington had forced her into something that had needed doing. In London, her involvement with Rupert would have grown into a love-affair – one that destroyed his marriage and left him for ever torn in two; he wasn't resolute enough to begin a new life without being tortured by the past.

She went back to work, trying to catch up time lost during her aunt's visit, and grateful for the fact that there was less inducement for the moment to go wandering around the islands. The summer season was in full swing, and though accommodation for visitors was strictly and sensibly limited by the Duchy of Cornwall, the launches nevertheless chugged away from the quay each morning laden with holiday passengers going to spend the day on one of the other islands. Once the Pied Piper's call of the boats had been answered, quiet descended on Hugh Town until midday, when the *Scillonian* arrived with the day-trippers from Penzance. If the crossing had been calm, their few hours ashore were spent happily enough wandering around St Mary's; if not, they huddled forlornly inside the first café they came to, contemplating the horror of the return journey ahead.

With the afternoon of her visit to Fairhaven now changed, Anna had been able to avoid any more unsettling meetings with Hugo. The rearrangement had earned her a quizzical look from Hubner, but a slightly warmer smile from Judith Jackson if ever they chanced to meet in the grounds of Fairhaven. The painting lessons were now going with such a swing that the children had progressed to the point of handling paint themselves, and whenever possible Anna took them out of doors to sketch. She was constantly fascinated by the different results produced by children who were all looking at the same subject, and their wildly individual ways of realising what they saw in paint led to endless discussions with Peter Hubner after the class was over.

Anna enjoyed his friendship, and would have enjoyed it even more if she hadn't been troubled by the suspicion that he needed very little encouragement to think himself in love with her. She liked him too well to want to see him hurt, and carefully turned aside the hints he offered her. The limits that she set were accepted with good grace, and their friendship was mercifully free of the mixture of nervous excitement and irritation that Hugo McKay aroused in her. The Austrian's gentleness reminded her of Rupert, but he had self-disciplined strength as well.

It was noticeable, therefore, that walking back with her to the cottage after the lesson one afternoon, he was abstracted enough for Anna to ask if something was bothering him.

"Something . . . yes," he agreed slowly. "But my problem is that I don't know what the something is . . . yet. Have you had any trouble with Denise Trotter, Anna?"

"If she's a rather pretty, sulky child, with a mane of black hair, yes, I have. She wanted my attention all the time, and became fretful the moment I spoke to anyone else. Then rather to my relief she suddenly stopped coming."

"That sounds like Denise. She's fifteen, by the way – older than the other children, in fact older than we normally accept; but so much in need of help that we bent the rules in her case. Now it begins to look as if we made a mistake."

His face when Anna glanced at him was so grave and troubled that she went on. "Tell me – if it helps to talk about it," she suggested gently.

"Well, the truth is that I'm at a loss! I thought I was making good progress with her, but now something's going wrong. The sort of life she's had was bound to make her precocious, and it isn't unusual for such a girl to get a fixation on the doctor who's treating her. I can normally handle that easily enough, but I'd swear she's under some other influence at the moment . . . still, I shall probably finish up taking the problem to Hugo, as we all do."

Anna made no comment on a solution that wasn't open to her personally – her chief problem lay in trying to avoid the man, not in seeking him out. It was difficult enough in the smallness of Hugh Town, but the problem was made worse by the fact that his most direct route into the centre lay past her own front door. She had to be constantly on the watch to avoid running into him along the narrow neck of land separating St Mary's Pool on the north side of the island from Porth Cressa Bay on the south. It was at Porth Cressa, she discovered accidentally, that he now braved the cold Atlantic water for his early-morning swim. Walking there with Ulysses one morning she almost bumped into him, fortunately staring seaward as he towelled himself dry. She quickly dragged her reluctant animal away, but the image of Hugo's powerful brown body stayed in her mind long after she'd given it leave to disappear.

She was careful never to discuss him with Harriet, but her red-headed friend wasn't so reticent. Harriet disliked his connection with Judith Jackson and made no bones about saying so.

"I'm not criticising her professionally, Anna," she said one day. "Peter says she makes a good job of being Fairhaven's matron; in fact, she's more than capable of running a large London hospital. I just wish she'd go away and run one! I don't want to see Hugo end up marrying her, and it seems to me he's drifting into a situation he won't be able to put into reverse. He's a sitting-duck for a woman who's clever at making him feel he's her only prop and stay; and Judith *is* clever, damn her – I have to give her that. Robin snorts at the idea, insisting that only strong inclinations would tempt Hugo into matrimony again, in which case there'd be nothing for us to do except make the best of it; but I pray it doesn't come to that."

On balance, Anna thought, Harriet was nearer the truth than Robin, who underestimated a determined woman's ability to get what she wanted. Her own contact with Hugo was limited to brief glimpses of him in church, where he looked tired still, and not particularly happy. Alice, friend and confidante of Morag Robertson, seemed to supply the reason. She reported that he'd offered himself for duty abroad again and had been rejected as still not sufficiently fit. Anna supposed that he was irritated by the time it was taking for a physician to heal himself, as well as growing bored by having nothing to do. She aired this theory to Alice, who firmly shook her head.

"The doctor's not idle," she said positively. "Seeing they're short-handed at the hospital, with visitors falling in and out of boats and giving themselves sunstroke, he's in the surgery most of the time, helping out."

Mrs Pengelly's further statement that he was a prince among men also seemed better not argued with. Anna agreed with a smile, and resolutely ignored the longing hidden in her heart to give him whatever would remove the sadness she occasionally glimpsed in his thin face.

Eight

Alice's morning visits now usually began with a lament about the visitors, and certainly there were as many of them as St Mary's could conveniently absorb. As a result, Anna's own off-island exploring was restricted to Saturdays. Then, she'd discovered, was the traditional change-over time for hotels and boarding houses during the holiday season, and Saturday was the one day of the week when the motor launches were likely to be pleasantly empty. On such a Saturday she set off with Ulysses as usual, food and sketching things in a knapsack, for a place she hadn't yet found a chance to visit – the famous subtropical gardens of Tresco Abbey, which Harriet had insisted were at their most spectacular and colourful in midsummer.

It was a calm, perfect morning, with the pearly haze lying over the sea that indicated blazing heat to come. The noticeboard on the quay advertising the morning's sailings said that it was the *Black Swan*'s turn to go to Tresco, but she was still hunting for it among the flotilla of boats moored against the sea-wall when her knapsack was suddenly lifted out of her hand. Hugo stood smiling down at her, dressed

96

for comfort rather than smartness in faded shorts and a disreputable old cotton sweater.

"Morning, m'dear," he said in a passable imitation of a local boatman. "Where'm you makin' for, then?"

"Tresco," she said truthfully, too conscious of him to be able to think of prevaricating.

"Splendid," Hugo answered in his normal voice. "It's on my way, I'll drop you off."

He disappeared down the steps and jumped into a small boat bobbing against the wall. Ulysses, treacherously glad to see a friend, bounded after him and, since her belongings as well as her dog had now gone, Anna had no choice but to follow them. She climbed over the side in a silence not intended to conceal the fact that she resented the doctor's high-handed ways. He took no notice of her injured air, carefully nosed the boat clear of the waiting huddle of launches, and then headed out across the channel towards Tresco. The island was near enough to be clearly visible ahead of them – a thin, pure line of white sand, backed by the dark green of pine woods, and the sea-pinks' wonderful splashes of colour. She heard Hugo give a small sigh of pleasure and the sound enticed her into glancing at him. It was a mistake, because he'd been waiting for her to do just that, and she found it impossible to resist the smile that tipped up the corners of his mouth.

"That's better," he said gently. "You've reminded me for the last five minutes of one of those ladies who modelled for ship's figureheads, glaring balefully out to sea!"

She had to grin at the idea, but quickly returned to watching the island ahead of them; it would never do for the over-confident doctor to know that far from feeling baleful, she was deeply content. This brief journey across a hyacinth-coloured sea was a moment stolen out of time. Truthful with herself, though not with him, she knew how much the moment was enriched for being shared with the man who sat opposite her, idly holding the tiller of the little boat. While she gazed at Tresco with fierce concentration, and wrestled inwardly with this discovery, Hugo took advantage of a rare opportunity to look at *her*. He caught glimpses of her much more often than she supposed, but she was always in the act of disappearing over the skyline. Now, snared for the moment in his boat, she couldn't run away on her beautiful tanned legs. She turned suddenly and caught him out in a leisurely inspection but he was unabashed, and it was she who looked away again.

"Where are you going after Tresco?" she managed to ask, and noticed that the question did seem to disconcert him. "You were going to drop me on your way," she added as a reminder.

"Anywhere could have been said to be on my way because I hadn't quite made up my mind," he recovered himself enough to point out. "But I've decided now – I shall spend the day on Tresco."

This time she wasn't inclined to smile. He'd tricked her into coming with him, and all her careful plans to keep out of his way had been brought to nothing by the deception. Her set expression made him stare at her.

"Don't look so severe. Morag made it clear that

I wasn't wanted at home this morning; she'd got an orgy of spring-cleaning in mind. I could spend the day alone, of course, but I'd much rather you let me spend it with you."

She heard wistfulness as well as amusement in his voice, and had to steel her heart against it by thinking of Judith Jackson.

"I'm not here to idle my time away – I came with a purpose – to see the gardens."

"Excellent. Ulysses and I will walk a respectful ten paces behind, carrying your impedimenta while you examine the botanical specimens."

She looked at his solemn mouth, saw the smile lurking in his eyes, and capitulated disgracefully without another shot being fired.

They did indeed visit the gardens, and it soon became clear that Hugo knew a good deal more about them than she did.

"Don't expect anything too trim and manicured," he warned her as they climbed up the sandy track from the jetty. "A lot of the trees and plants are exotic – best left rampant, exactly as they'd grow where they really belong. Augustus Smith, who first made a home here out of the crumbling remains of a Benedictine priory – the present Abbey in fact – had to begin by clearing a wilderness of heather and gorse. He got his first plantings from the Royal Botanical Gardens at Kew, but the islanders were very energetic seafarers in the nineteenth century and they were soon bringing him back specimens from all over the world."

Anna looked at the sand through which they were trudging, and marvelled out loud that anything but thistles and sea-pinks could have been induced to grow in it.

"That wasn't old Augustus's problem," Hugo said, shaking his head. "His main worry was how to shelter his precious plants from the winds that sweep across the island, and it's still a problem for the present-day owners – that's why you'll see windbreaks of pine here and there. But the gardens have become deservedly famous."

They were quite as exotic as Hugo had claimed, and would have been breathtaking in any circumstances, but Anna's eye was continually drawn by some beautiful combination of trees seen against a theatrical backdrop of indigo-coloured sea and azure sky. 'Old Augustus' had known a thing or two about laying out a garden.

At last the sheltered grounds became too hot for comfort, and she had to confess that her thirst for botanical curiosities was being swamped by the different need of a cool drink and a seat in some shady spot. Hugo led her to a small deserted beach on the western side of the island, undiscovered by the people the *Black Swan* would have brought over. They had the tiny paradise entirely to themselves – a curving sickle of white sand, lapped by sapphire water that turned to emerald where it ran shallow over the shore. But for all its beautiful colour, it was still Atlantic water. Anna's swim was brief and brisk, and she was soon dressed again in shirt and shorts. Hugo and Ulysses, made of sterner stuff, continued to cavort together in the water while she spread out their combined lunch in the shade of the pine trees fringing the beach.

"The Fortunate Isles at their most idyllic," Hugo said when he and his friend had been induced to come and sit down. "But what about the other times, Anna? How do you feel about the islands when we're shrouded in fog, or battered by gales and rain? Do you find yourself hankering for city life then?"

"Not even then," she answered after some thought. "When I left London I believed I'd grown to love it, but now I should hate to go back. I seem to have become a fully-fledged islander, and since Aunt Agatha has been generous enough to make me a gift of the cottage there's no reason why I shouldn't stay and do my work here."

"You've learned to live happily without the things London undoubtedly has to offer," Hugo commented. "And I know you've found friends here, but you mentioned once that you'd had to leave a particular friend behind. Am I allowed to ask about him, or is it still too painful?"

She looked up to find his glance on her. A lie would have been out of the question even if she hadn't wanted him to know the truth.

"Not painful now, though it certainly *was*," she admitted quietly. "I couldn't imagine then that I'd ever stop missing Rupert, but I've even got to the point of feeling grateful that he didn't have to choose between me and his wife."

She watched Hugo gently scratching the one spot on Ulysses' back that her clever hound could never reach himself, then decided that she might fairly ask a question of her own. "What about you? This is a

101

long way from *your* native heath. Don't you ever get homesick?"

"I don't think I have a native heath any longer," he said ruefully. "It ill becomes a Highlander to say so, but I've spent so much of my life away from Scotland, at school, college, or in one hospital after another, that I don't seem to belong there any more. For the moment I'm committed to going back to Africa when they'll have me, but eventually I'd like to finish up here. Doctoring on these islands must be wonderfully varied, and enjoyable for as long as a visiting GP can manage the rather athletic landfalls required when the tide isn't right!"

After lunch Anna inevitably pulled out her sketch-book and sat making quick line-drawings of the gulls who came to give an aerial acrobatic display in return for the last remnants of lunch. Ulysses sat so close to his mistress while the performance was going on that Hugo eventually commented on the fact.

"If it didn't seem so unlikely I'd be inclined to say that Ulysses is trying to make himself invisible for once."

She gave her dog a consoling pat. "He's wary of gulls at the moment. We were over on Gugh the other day and he didn't immediately realise that he wasn't welcome on their nesting rocks. I didn't realise it either, or we'd have gone another way, but he came back showing a very undignified burst of speed, pursued by a flock of very angry black-backs!"

Hugo sat in contented silence for a while, and then suddenly fell fast asleep. With his dark hair drying roughly about his face, he looked younger and more vulnerable – very sketchable, in fact, but Anna resisted the temptation for fear that he might wake and catch her at it. Finally she laid down her pencil to wander with Ulysses along the shore, and when they got back Hugo was awake again.

"Silly of me," he said quietly. "I didn't mean to waste any of this lovely day by sleeping through it; though on second thoughts perhaps it was just as well."

She decided to read nothing into that remark in case she read it wrongly. "I think so, too . . . You still look like a man with sleep to be caught up on."

His eyes lingered on her for a moment. "It isn't quite what I meant. A doctor is expressly forbidden to seduce his patients, and although you aren't my patient, strictly speaking, I should be breaking the spirit of our code, if not its letter, by doing what I should greatly like to do."

His voice was still half-amused, but she wasn't misled now, and awareness of their complete isolation washed over her. They could have been alone on a desert island – Adam and Eve not yet dispossessed of Eden. She dragged her eyes away from his, and stared instead at the tell-tale hands clenched hard at his sides. He managed a wry smile, but his voice was ragged when he spoke again. "We'd better rejoin the rest of the human race, I think, before I consign Hippocrates and his very inconvenient oath to oblivion!"

She set about packing up their scattered belongings, hoping he wouldn't notice the labour she was making of it. Naked longing had almost won a moment ago, but that wasn't what made her hands tremble. Her own bitter disappointment, she was having to realise, lay simply in the fact that that longing had failed. Hugo's self-control had had something to do with it, but she feared that Judith had had much more. If it had been his beautiful blonde colleague here with him, *she* wouldn't have been sedately packing up the picnic-basket. Anna told herself to be grateful to escape an entanglement that would be probably more ruinous than her broken affair with Rupert, but the sense of rejection remained; she wasn't what he really wanted, even though he'd been tempted for a moment or two. The knowledge lay between them now, souring the lovely pleasure of the day.

Back in Hugo's small boat, she expected to see him head straight for St Mary's, but he turned the nose eastward instead, skirted St Martin's, and spent the next hour showing her the birds that made their home on the exposed, fantastically-shaped granite rocks that were called the Eastern Isles. There were clusters of small kittiwakes starring the rocks like grey and white flowers; shags and cormorants perched on every pinnacle, holding out their black wings as if to dry, and scarlet-nosed puffins swooped down to skim their supper from the water. Last, and best of all, a colony of seals decided to offer them a final, captivating show of clowning.

At last, when Hugo judged that the easy companionship of the morning had been restored, he steered towards the harbour at St Mary's, through the cool softness of the summer evening. They parted company almost without anything being said, and Anna was grateful for it. The day was already too full of things that needed to be thought about and stored away.

It didn't occur to her that their return to Hugh Town was being watched with interest by the row of citizens who sat on the sea-wall taking the evening air. She climbed up the steps to the quay happily unaware that one old sailor, pleased by the doctor's neat handling of his boat, was pointing this out to the beautiful, fair-haired woman who'd come to stand at his side.

"I 'spec 'ee wanted to impress his young leddy," the old man told Judith with a knowing grin. "Did the same me'self back a year or two!"

She gave a thin smile and walked away, not interested in his reminiscences; there were urgent matters of her own to think about.

Nine

A week after the visit to Tresco, Anna put down her brush one evening with a sigh of relief and dropped a thankful kiss on the end of Ulysses' nose. It had been a long, final day's work, but she'd been determined not to stop until the Grimms' illustrations were finished. They were done at last, and though they would need careful examination after a night's sleep, she felt content with them; very little, if anything, would need re-doing.

The big folder on her table contained four months' meticulous work, and the only sure way of getting it to London undamaged would be to take it herself. She was surprised to discover how much she hated that necessity. Having to leave her house and her dog was a reasonable enough objection, but less rationally she was aware of a kind of superstitious dread. She wanted *not* to have to visit London – it could be taken in the stride of seasoned habitués, no doubt, but she wasn't one of them any longer; life went at a different pace in Hugh Town. Still, the completed illustrations had to be delivered, and her materials were getting dangerously low.

There was another need as well – a wardrobe

originally intended for a working girl in London wouldn't quite match the requirements of an island winter.

Harriet, when asked if she could accommodate Ulysses for a couple of days, sounded genuinely delighted at the idea of having yet another inmate added to her assorted household.

"It's only so that I can go and come back more quickly," Anna explained to the dog who sat beside her listening to this conversation. "You'd hate being put into a crate to go by helicopter, and it would mean a very slow journey by boat and train."

He accepted the proposition without any fuss, and allowed himself to be made much of by Emily and Liza when Anna deposited him with the Graysons the next afternoon. She had booked herself on an early-morning flight, and had no intention of spending more than two nights with Aunt Agatha in London; but she trudged home after saying goodbye to Ulysses with the feeling that her world had suddenly come to an end. It was an effort to pack a suitcase; even more of an effort to prepare food she didn't feel in the least like eating.

In the middle of beating eggs to make herself an omelette she was interrupted by a knock at the door. She went to open it, guessing who would be there, but it wasn't Peter Hubner standing on her doorstep, nor Alice, Morag, or anyone else she might have had the slightest expectation of seeing. The man who waited there, smiling uncertainly, was Rupert Neville, and for a moment she was transfixed with shock, helpless to say or do anything at all.

107

"I-I don't believe it," she murmured unsteadily. "Rupert . . . What in the world are you doing on St Mary's?"

"Hoping to be asked inside?" he suggested tentatively.

Her face flushed with sudden colour for the shame of knowing that her immediate reaction had been one of strong dismay. It wasn't what he would have felt entitled to expect, even if he'd merely called on her in London. She held the door open and gestured him inside.

"Sorry, Rupert . . . I expect I'm overcome, and my wits have gone begging."

She led him into the sitting-room and they stood looking at one another, measuring what the months of separation had done to both of them.

"It's lovely to see you, but I still don't understand how you come to be here," she said at last, when the silence threatened to grow awkward.

He ran his hands through a mop of fair hair, making it more rumpled than ever. It was a gesture she remembered vividly, and it had the effect of making him seem less of a stranger.

"I know you meant me to do nothing after I got your letter, Anna, but I simply couldn't leave things like that. There had to be a reason for your disappearance, and I could guess what it was. I had to see for myself that you were all right. Don't be cross with me for coming."

She was bound to reassure him. "Of course I'm not cross . . . just trying to work out how you knew where to find me."

"It's a long story. After I'd seen your aunt – who quite rightly refused to be forthcoming – I had the luck to locate the doctor who treated you in hospital. He wouldn't commit himself either, to begin with, though he did admit that he knew where you were going. But he promised to take what he called 'local advice' in the matter and eventually decided to confess that you'd come to St Mary's. I remembered you once mentioning your aunt's cottage here, so I simply asked a couple of people where it was."

The local advice could only have come from Hugo, Anna thought wearily. There was no limit, apparently, to the extent that he and his friend, Dr Redfern, were prepared to interfere in other people's lives, in the mistaken belief that they knew what was good for them. As a result of their well-meaning conspiracy, she was caught in a situation she found well-nigh intolerable. Rupert's visit was all wrong. A sad waste of time and energy for him, and what felt like a sad awkwardness for her. It was strange and disconcerting to know that a visit she'd have been overjoyed by a few months ago now seemed an embarrassing anticlimax.

"I really am all right," she managed to say at last. "Parting company with Carrington's was a blow, but the worst part of *that* was discovering that people I'd worked with for a long time couldn't resist earning a few good marks from the Chairman by confirming what he wanted to hear. I celebrated my departure from the company by sliding down a flight of steps and knocking myself out. Afterwards dear Aunt Agatha saw the mess I was in and had the brilliant idea of sending me here. I now work freelance in the loveliest surroundings imaginable, among people who have become my good friends." She smiled as she came to the end of the story, relieved that it now seemed to have more to do with Carrington's than with themselves; but Rupert's face – London-pale and tired after the long journey – needed something else. "Perhaps I'm more all right than you are," she added gently.

He thought it was the truth. Now that she'd recovered from the shock of seeing him, he could observe clearly the sea-change in the lonely, work-obsessed girl he'd known in London. Simply dressed in a striped cotton shirt and skirt, and tanned by the sea air and sunshine, she looked not only beautiful but serene now as well.

"How are *you*?" she asked when he made no attempt to answer her oblique question.

"I manage, more or less. But I miss you rather badly." Then the voice he'd tried to make casual suddenly changed. "My darling, I'm sorry it was all such a bloody mess. I got a letter from Desmond while I was in New York. It was wonderfully bland and reassuring, with only a tiny hint of the iron hand in the velvet glove. I could have killed him then, but by the time I'd read that damned letter for the tenth time I realised that most of what he said was true . . ."

His voice broke and died, and Anna went to the side-table where her uncle's heavy decanters still stood. With whisky poured, she came back to hand him a glass. "Rupert . . . don't go on agonising about it, please. It's over now; not something to be forgotten entirely, but no longer what we live with every day. I thought I hated Desmond Carrington too, but I don't any longer; he did what he believed was right for his daughter and his grandchildren. I'm not sure he didn't genuinely reckon he was even doing what was best for you."

Rupert gave a grimace of pain, and took a gulp of his drink, leaving her to find something else to say. "What about the children?" she asked after a moment. "Are they all right?"

His strained face finally broke into a smile. "They're my only joy, Anna. Funny, sweet and naughty by turns – worth what they've cost *me*, but I had to be sure about you."

She felt suddenly glad after all that he'd wanted to pay her this farewell visit. There were better ways of ending a relationship than the brutal slash of Desmond Carrington's hatchet. But she still clung to things professional. "I'm really all right – in fact I'm doing so well that I shall end up grateful to the Chairman for dispensing with my services! Incidentally, I'm due to go to London tomorrow morning to see a publisher. We could travel back together."

She realised that it left undealt with the matter of the night in between. Rupert had almost certainly come expecting the sort of welcome that would lead them naturally into bed together; she had no idea how to begin explaining that it wasn't going to happen. But to her huge relief he grasped the nettle himself.

"Anna, don't look so anxious! Even if I hadn't made a fresh start with Cynthia that I can't renege on, I have the feeling that you've moved on from where we left off. You don't need me any more – am I right?"

Her nod answered him, but she wanted more than anything else at that moment to make him understand how the change in her had come about.

"It's no wonder I wasn't popular at Carrington's – I can see easily enough from this distance what an awkward stand-offish creature I must have seemed; but *you*, dear Rupert, refused to be put off! It's in the past now, but I shall always be grateful. Thanks largely to you, I can manage on my own now."

He looked at her in silence for a moment, and then put down his glass with a brisk air. "I'd better go and do something about finding a room for the night."

This time Anna shook her head. "Hopeless, I fear. It's high season here and you could comb the entire town without finding an attic available. I'll make up the bed in the spare room for you." She put down her own glass and smiled at him. "Supper first, though. I was just getting it when you arrived."

This time she didn't even get as far as the kitchen before another caller knocked at the front door. She opened it on a visitor almost as unexpected as Rupert had been – Judith Jackson hadn't shown the slightest interest in calling on her before. But more unwelcome than the sight of *her* faintly smiling on the doorstep was the looming shape behind her of Hugo McKay.

"We called to check up on you," Judith said with a charmingly anxious air. "Peter was worried about you . . . said you were most unlike yourself this afternoon. He seemed so convinced that you were sickening for something that I promised to make sure you were all right."

"It's kind of you, but Peter must have been imagining things. I'm fine." Anna hoped she sounded grateful but firm.

Of Hugo she took no notice at all, beyond offering him the briefest of nods. Short of shutting the door in the face of her visitors she could think of nothing else to do that would discourage them from lingering. Courtesy seemed to require that she should invite them in, but she was deeply reluctant to do so. She hesitated and was lost, because Judith stepped confidently into the hall, apparently still hell-bent on playing her role of ministering angel. Hugo, perforce, followed her, even though he'd registered Anna's keen desire to see them go. The sight of Rupert getting to his feet in the sitting-room seemed to explain her lack of welcome, and even brought Judith to an embarrassed halt.

"An old friend from London – Rupert Neville," Anna explained reluctantly. "Judith Jackson and Dr McKay, Rupert."

She offered the newcomers drinks, concealing a strong inclination to weep or scream at the perversity of fate. Rupert made laboured conversation with Judith, while the doctor nursed his glass and looked as if he'd been penned there much against his will. When he did finally bestir himself to say something it was only to ask an abrupt question.

"Where's Ulysses, Anna?"

"I left him with the Graysons. I have to go to London tomorrow," she answered with equal brevity.

"And you, Mr Neville," said Hugo, turning to the man he'd so far completely ignored. "Are you staying on St Mary's for a while?"

"No – I'm afraid not, much as I should like to. I shall be going back with Anna tomorrow."

"Nice for you both," Hugo commented smoothly. Then he swallowed the remainder of his whisky in one quick gulp and turned to Judith. "We must go . . . we're probably intruding."

His face was the face of a stranger – detached, bored, even faintly inimical. Their relationship, chequered since the very day of her arrival at St Mary's, was now – his expression confirmed it – irretrievably dead. The lovely shared day on Tresco would never be repeated, and the memory of it could be thrown on the rubbish heap. Hugo's face said all too clearly that he was sickened by the lie she'd offered him; her relationship with Rupert Neville wasn't over and done with; she was still clinging to a love affair that was not only shabby but hopeless.

Not hearing a word of Judith's flow of bright chatter, Anna smiled and struggled with an insane urge to shout the truth at Hugo. She felt absurdly betrayed by his failure to understand it without being told, even while she acknowledged to herself that anyone else coming upon Rupert there would have put exactly the same construction on his visit.

Hugo finally succeeded in dragging Judith away and, at the third attempt, Anna managed to get supper cooked; she even ate some of it. By comparison with what had gone before, the rest of the evening seemed mercifully dull. She listened to Rupert's news of events at Carrington's, marvelling that she felt no real interest in them; but perhaps he felt the same about the recent work she showed him. It was a relief when the time came to show him to the spare bedroom, and she felt as exhausted as when she'd first arrived at the cottage.

Despite fatigue, she spent a sleepless night considering the evening's revelations. She would part company with Rupert, almost certainly for good this time, feeling only gratitude towards him on her own account; if anxiety about *her* had troubled him it could be put away now, but she was left fearing that the future might be an on-going struggle for him; God send Cynthia Neville kindness and generosity enough to patch their marriage together again.

She fixed her mind on Rupert and his wife rather than permitting it to fasten on a problem of her own. The evening had also been painful in an unexpected way, presenting her with a comparison she couldn't help making. Beside Hugo McKay, Rupert had looked wan and ineffectual, and even the gentleness she'd once prized in him now didn't seem sufficiently underlain with strength. But the revaluation was part of the cruel perversity of things; she knew the worth of the man who despised her – the evening had made *that* crystal clear as well.

There was another, though less important, irritant – an inconsistency thrown up by the disastrous evening. Simon Redfern's local information could only have come from Hugo, so why had he looked so displeased at finding Rupert with her?

*   *   *

Thankful for an eight a.m. flight that allowed her to get up soon after dawn, she woke her guest, got breakfast while he shaved, and having made them ready much too early, walked him round the town at a rate that the city man found strenuous. During the flight to Penzance and the long train journey to Paddington, she forced herself to talk normally, but she refused to let Rupert escort her to Aunt Agatha's. This time they knew their parting for what it was, and Anna realised fully what she'd refused to accept before – Desmond Carrington's handling of things had been more humane than she'd ever given him credit for. But Rupert's face as he stood waving to her from the taxi-rank looked so heart-breakingly sad that she sat in the taxi weeping for his loneliness.

Her forlorn appearance didn't go unnoticed when she arrived at her aunt's small house in Kensington, but apart from a more affectionate greeting than usual, Agatha Prescott made no comment on her niece's tragic expression.

The interview with her publishers after lunch went some way to restoring Anna's shattered spirits. They were complimentary about her work on the Grimms' illustrations – so much so that she plucked up the courage to delve into her folder again and bring out some of her Scillies sketches. Peter Hubner had been insistent that she bring them, but she handed them over diffidently, with only the suggestion of an Islands sketchbook – her drawings linked by passages of text that would touch briefly on local history and the individual flavour of each of the islands.

She watched the man in front of her turn the pages,

then go back and look at certain sketches again. The expression on his face hinted only at polite interest and she waited for him to say that, charming as the drawings were, he really saw no future for them. Then he closed the folder very deliberately, and smiled at her for the first time in the course of their interview.

"Don't dare to offer them to anyone else," he finally commanded. "I want them myself – as complete as you can make them."

The prospect of earning money she scarcely needed in the present rosy state of her finances meant very little, but the text-writer she had in mind was Michael Harding, and the thought of being able to add a windfall to *his* exchequer made her grin for the first time since Rupert's knock had sounded at the cottage door.

"Now, what about the words?" the editor was asking briskly. "Can you manage them as well?"

She shook her head. "Not nearly enough local knowledge, or writing skill, but I know someone at Hugh Town who would do it beautifully if he'd agree."

She promised to have the completed illustrations ready in three months' time. It would mean another concentrated stint of work, but for that she felt grateful. She needed to be busy, not left with time to think about a faint, elusive vision glimpsed one day on Tresco; perdition would take her soul and chaos come again if she couldn't keep *that* out of her mind.

She spent the whole of the next day in an orgy of shopping. Fresh stocks of paint and paper would be needed more than ever now, and the fine materials she used were not easily come by in Hugh Town. There were clothes to buy, too – sturdy sweaters and a decent waterproof; Scillies winters weren't cold by mainland standards, but she knew enough about the islands' weather now to know that there would certainly be gales, and rain in plenty. Finally, she looked for presents to take back with her, and set off from Paddington the following morning surrounded by a heap of parcels and packages. Her visit had been rather enjoyable after all, but she was happy to be heading westward again. Whatever grief might lie in wait for her there, it was where she belonged now – it was her home.

A mid-afternoon flight from Penzance got her back to St Mary's in time to dump luggage at the cottage, then race up to the Garrison to share the children's tea and collect Ulysses. He caught sight of her walking through the courtyard and launched himself from the garden steps in a flying leap that all but knocked her flat.

"Do you think he looks thin, Anna?" Emily enquired anxiously when she could make herself heard above the noise he was now making. "We kept trying to make him eat, but he didn't seem to have the heart for it."

"Playing for sympathy," Anna said. "He looks the picture of health. Thank you, Emily dear, for taking care of him for me."

She was greeted by the Graysons, large and small, with a warmth that suggested she'd been long lost in foreign parts instead of absent for two days in

London. Then her presents caused a fresh outbreak of pandemonium until Harriet shooed the children into the garden, insisting that she wanted Anna to herself for a bit. Her small freckled face was no longer smiling, and something in her manner suggested bad news held in reserve. She was so long in coming to the point that Anna finally asked what was troubling her, since something clearly was.

"It's Hugo," Harriet admitted tragically.

"You – you mean he's ill again?" Anna asked over the fear that seemed to be clutching at her heart.

"He's *been* ill again, but that isn't the trouble . . . At least, I suppose it might have had something to do with it."

"To do with *what?*" Anna commanded urgently. "Tell me, for pity's sake."

"Well, the dear fool's gone and got himself engaged to Judith Jackson," Harriet brought out with a rush. "The day you went to London he had another bout of fever, and I'm afraid Judith caught him at a weak moment – doing her ministering angel bit, no doubt."

There was a long silence while Anna examined her hands, pleased to find that they weren't shaking. "*You* may not like it, Harry dear, but we must suppose that Hugo does," she heard herself point out calmly.

"He's been trapped," her friend insisted, "like many a good man before him – by a beautiful, scheming woman. I could weep over it, if you want the truth."

Anna resisted the temptation to confess that *she* could have wept over it, too; but surely the ironic gods above were falling about with mirth – reminding

119

each other, between homeric gusts of laughter, that Miss Anna Carteret had been going to live in beautiful self-sufficiency, with no more hostages to fortune. She shared Harriet's dislike of Judith Jackson, but she knew that what she really struggled with was sheer, shaming jealousy of the woman who was going to be Hugo's new wife. He wasn't made stupid by kindness, would never have been led like a lamb to the slaughter if his heart hadn't inclined him in the direction of Judith.

It seemed necessary to make this clear to Harriet, because *her* interpretation of his engagement was not only wrong but somehow demeaning to him.

"You're being unfair," she said with a snap that made her friend stare. "The people who love Hugo seem to get absurdly proprietorial about him. Why not just admit that he prefers Judith to anyone else, even if *you* don't happen to like her?"

Harriet digested this suggestion in silence for a moment; then, after a glance at Anna's face, she smiled with all the sweetness that was her special grace.

"You're quite right, of course. We'll wish them happy, and keep our miserable resentments entirely to ourselves!"

Ten

With a book now commissioned and undertaken, Anna decided that she would wrench
her mind away from every distraction and begin to
concentrate only on the work in hand. The first thing
after her return from London, of course, must be to
call on Michael Harding. She outlined her Scillies
sketchbook idea and, having shown him some of the
material that might be included, sat watching him with
a hopeful air.

"You look like one of the robins in our garden,
defying us not to throw him a tit-bit!" he suggested.
"Do I take it that *you*'re needing to be thrown a
collaborator in this great venture?"

"I'm greatly in need of you," she admitted, too
disappointed by the lack of interest in his voice to
attempt finesse. "No one else that I'm acquainted
with here has the necessary skill or the knowledge.
In fact, without you, I doubt if the project can be
realised at all."

"Blackmail," he grunted, managing quite well not
to sound pleased.

Missing the smile that lurked behind his frown, she
began to pile her sketches together. "Then I won't

badger you. I'm sorry, Michael – it just seemed a nice idea, that's all."

His hand reached out to cover hers, and his face was suddenly alight with all the pleasure she'd hoped for. "I *love* the idea; in fact I'm tickled pink to be asked, but I couldn't resist teasing you! Now, I suppose there's a fiendish deadline? There always is in my experience."

"Not impossible: three months," she admitted with a grin of relief. "Three months' hard but happy work! Oh, I'm so glad you're *not* turning me down."

They settled to serious discussion of a programme that would allow them to meet the publisher's date, and Michael suggested that consultations should be at Anna's cottage in future. It would save her unnecessary leg-work, but also allow them – he explained with a smile as his sister came into the room – to escape Elizabeth's piano pupils who made his own home hideous during daylight hours.

Anna paid her usual visit to Fairhaven that afternoon, but she stayed talking afterwards to Peter Hubner; he was the original instigator of the book and had to be told about it. At last she went back to the room in which her afternoon's work with the children had been left to dry, but stopped short with a gasp at the sight of it. What had been a delicate study of a gorse and honeysuckle-covered headland jutting out into blue water was now an obscene mess down which crimson paint still dribbled sluggishly. Hubner, waiting in the doorway, heard her small groan and rushed across the room.

"What is it, Anna? Are you unwell?" But the rest was bitten off as he saw what she was staring at. "Oh, my God!"

She carefully blotted the wet paint, scarcely aware of that first instinctive reaction; but the red-daubed rag in her hand prompted the inevitable question: "Who would do such a thing?"

In his face she saw anger that the vandalising of anything lovely was bound to arouse, but there was something else as well – sadness, she thought, for a culprit he believed he could identify. "I expect you'll say that who it was doesn't matter," she added quietly. "It's *why* that's important, isn't it?"

He locked the ruined painting away in his study without answering and then walked back with her to the cottage as usual.

"Perhaps you've guessed that I'm afraid Denise Trotter is to blame," he said as they went along. "I told you that I was going to consult Hugo about her, but I didn't in the end. Fairhaven's problems are what *I'm* supposed to cope with, and in any case Hugo hasn't been well enough to be bothered with anything just lately."

He made the explanation sound convincing, and saw no point in burdening Anna with his real reason for not discussing Denise with Hugo. It was one thing to be certain himself that Judith was deliberately undermining his own influence with an unstable and unhappy adolescent; it was quite another to tell this to Judith's fiancé, who also happened to be his closest friend.

"I saw Denise early this afternoon," Anna admitted

reluctantly. "She was in the cloakroom when I arrived, but just went on preening herself in front of the mirror. I was ignored, but *meant* to notice the sundress she was wearing; it looked expensive and much too sophisticated for a girl of her age."

"One of Judith's cast-offs," Hubner explained with regret. "We had a sharp difference of opinion about it this morning. She thinks it is doing the child a kindness to give her the sort of things she craves. Being a mere man, I'm apparently unable to understand that, whether I'm a psychiatrist or not!"

Anna glanced at his troubled face and hesitated over the wording of her next sentence. "I suppose I'm also meant to notice that Denise's hostility is directed at *me*; if it's our friendship that she resents, would it help if I didn't come to Fairhaven any more?"

"Probably, in the short term, but it's no solution to the problem. We can't leave Denise with that sort of victory, and in any case why should the other children be penalised? They love your lessons. No, please don't stay away. I shall find some other way of dealing with Denise."

"You said Hugo had been unwell," she said next, with difficulty. "Is he still?"

"Better now, I think, but another bout of fever, when he thought he'd got the damned bug out of his system, has depressed him. He's too good a doctor not to know that his chances of being allowed back in Africa are beginning to look slim, but he loved working there." Hubner's face broke into a rueful grin. "He's like a bear with a sore head at the moment!

Even friends as old as Harriet and me scarcely dare speak to him."

It was tempting to blame it on his engagement, but unfair, Anna told herself firmly. She had no proof that Judith was trying to isolate him from other people so as to leave him more dependant on herself. In fact she knew of one old friend whom Hugo was certainly still visiting. She'd been recruited herself for this same duty by Michael Harding, and now spent half an hour most afternoons talking to Ben Trevithian, an old boatman who was slowly dying of cancer. Ben had steadfastly refused to leave the waterside cottage he'd always lived in, and, knowing that Hugo was looking after him, the Island doctors had given up trying to persuade him to end his days in hospital.

Anna knew of Hugo's visits because the old man often talked about him – in terms that he might well have used of his own son. But it was some time before Hugo learned of her own calls at the cottage. One day he had thought to comment on the bowl of exquisitely arranged wild flowers that now always decorated his friend's bedside table, and Ben's worn face broke into an entrancing smile.

"My new girlfriend brings them for me. Brings her dog as well. Queerest-looking animal you ever saw, with a name to match. What do you think she calls him – Ulysses!"

"I'm acquainted with Ulysses," Hugo admitted, but he saw no reason to confess that he knew anything at all about the dog's owner.

He scarcely saw her himself, except for occasional glimpses in church, from which she always hurried away quickly afterwards. It was something to be thankful for. The recollection of his call on her with Judith was still branded across his mind and he made himself relive it again whenever the memory of a day spent on Tresco came back to haunt him. How close he'd come then to making an abject fool of himself; how ludicrous had been his belief in Anna Carteret. The only thing to do now was to forget her and concentrate on Judith instead. He was too perceptive not to be aware that their engagement had dismayed his friends, valiantly though they tried to conceal the fact. Well, he couldn't claim even to himself that Judith was the woman he might have dreamed of finding. But he needed a wife, hoped for a family, and had some vague but insistent idea that by making Judith happy he could wipe away the sadness of his failure with Kirstie. He was older and wiser now, and would make this marriage work. Judith had visited him the day after Anna returned to London with the slight, fair-haired man who'd seemed so damnably at home in her sitting-room. He was shaking with fever and feeling suicidally depressed, and Judith had never looked more coolly beautiful or been more kind.

"What do *you* want out of life?" he'd asked her suddenly. "To rise to the top of the nursing profession?"

"Certainly, if I have to stay in it," she'd answered with the honesty he liked in her. "I don't see the point of being an also-ran. But I'd have been happier helping William – making a home for him; giving him children."

The simple confession hadn't been made, Hugo

126

felt sure, to remind him that he was involved in her loss. It merely echoed what was in his own mind – they'd both come to grief and been left lonely.

"I'm not William, my dear, but shall *we* try for the family instead?" The words had suddenly spoken themselves, unpremeditated but seeming inevitable when she answered him.

"Oh, yes, Hugo, yes, please!" Her usually guarded expression was warmed by a flush of happiness that made her look young again, and, seeing the transformation, he'd been content with what he'd done. He'd even smiled at the thought of Agatha Prescott; she wouldn't need to nag him any more about finding a wife!

In the following days he avoided his friends and devoted his time to Judith instead. He refused to admit to himself that it seemed hard to feel happy in her company; happiness would come with practice, or at least acceptance would. But whether it did or not he must appear at ease, and convince everyone else that he was a man delighted with his chosen lot.

It was Anna who accidentally witnessed a demonstration of this determination when she was out with Ulysses on Garrison one evening. The grassy dells there seemed to have been fashioned specially for lovers, and Judith was being thoroughly kissed when a peremptory bark from up above interrupted the proceedings. Hugo lifted his head to see Ben's 'queer-looking' animal watching them with interest. Behind him, dark hair blowing in the cliff-top breeze,

Anna stared down at them for a moment, then called sharply to the dog and walked away.

Her stroll ended as always on the shore in front of the lifeboat station, so that Ulysses could make his usual pretence of dashing at the small waves that creamed against the sand. It was a game he played unwearyingly every evening, and he was playing it now when a tall figure loomed out of the dusk.

"So you're back from London, Anna," Hugo said affably. "Alone, may one ask, or is the delightful Mr Neville in residence again?"

She detected anger beneath the smoothness of his voice, and guessed the reason – he'd resented being caught with Judith, behaving like any hot-blooded village lad. But his question roused anger in return, swamping the guard she kept upon herself.

"I'm alone, as it happens. But I fail to understand why you should have seemed so surprised to find Rupert with me at the cottage that evening. After all, it was you who advised Simon Redfern to tell Rupert where to find me – a piece of interference that I haven't forgiven you for."

"I did *what*?" Hugo almost shouted.

"Your friend consulted you after Aunt Agatha refused to tell Rupert I was here. She had decided quite correctly *not* to interfere."

But the expression on Hugo's face told her now that he hadn't been involved either; however Rupert's visit had come about, it hadn't been inspired by the angry man in front of her.

"I haven't discussed you with Simon since before

you first arrived on St Mary's," he said more quietly, with complete conviction.

She managed a little shrug. "Well, it doesn't matter now, but I couldn't imagine who else he could have talked to."

Hugo's drawn face finally broke into a smile. "You mean that you can't think of anyone else who would barge into your affairs in the free and easy way you seem to think I do!"

"It doesn't matter," she said again tiredly. "Nor does what I'm going to say next, but I'll say it to set the record straight. Rupert *wasn't* in residence, as you so tactfully put it. He stayed one night at the cottage because I couldn't turn him out into the street, but he slept in the spare room by himself. You can believe that or not as you feel inclined."

A little silence followed this speech. Hugo broke it at last, sounding no longer angry, only immeasurably sad. "Put your fists down, Anna. I believe you even though I marvel at Neville's self-restraint!"

She told herself that it was the moment to say a dignified good-night and walk away, but her feet seemed rooted to the spot. Some magnetic attraction operated again between them, holding them immobile. But she was saved by the memory of the scene she'd interrupted earlier.

"I haven't congratulated you on your engagement. How remiss! Am I right in thinking that the wedding is . . . is imminent?"

Even in the gathering darkness she could see the glint of rueful amusement in his eyes. "And *that* card, I'm afraid, takes the trick!"

She was rescued finally by Ulysses, prancing up to make much of his friend.

"Take her home, old chap," he instructed the dog, "and keep her out of trouble if you can."

Eleven

The summer died slowly in a succession of golden days which always began and ended in a ghostly sea mist. The visitors got scarcer week by week, and their disappearance was the signal for the islanders to go back to their other traditional concern – the production of early spring flowers for the mainland market. By some annual, seasonal transmutation, sea-faring men who'd spent the entire summer on the water now laid up their boats and went back to the land. First the tall windbreak hedges of veronica and escallonia had to be repaired – they were needed to shelter the pocket-handkerchief-sized fields from the gales that swept over them in winter. Then the soil was turned over, and the bulbs sorted and replanted for another growing season. All manner of spring flowers flourished, but Anna was told repeatedly that the pride of the Scillies was the beautiful *Soleil d'Or* narcissus that grew there more straight and tall and fragrant than anywhere else on earth. For the flower-growers it was the 'Sols' that lay closest to their hearts.

She was happy to see the islands emptying again; beautiful though they were in the setting of the summer-coloured seas, some of the magic was lost when it had to be shared with crowds of strangers. Being a resident now, who didn't depart with the shortening days, she rejoiced to see the tide of visitors gradually ebbing away.

The island sketchbook was coming on well, but it meant spending long hours out of doors gathering as much material as possible before the fine weather broke. Then, over picnic suppers in the kitchen, she and Michael Harding haggled, argued and eventually agreed about what should go into the book and what should be discarded.

But despite the pressure of work, she was careful not to neglect the children at Fairhaven. For as long as the weather allowed, she took them out to sketch, often combining their lesson with her own search for material. In fact, she found them a positive help, sometimes spotting, with a viewpoint different from her own, things that she might otherwise have missed. Their own resulting sketches were so fresh and vivid that the idea of an exhibition of them suddenly occurred to her. Peter Hubner liked her enthusiasm too much to reveal his doubt that people would see anything to interest them in the children's work. Robin Grayson, enrolled by Anna in the task of getting the exhibition organised in his school, was happy to help, and more optimistic than Hubner; of course the people of Hugh Town would turn up – they were too kind not to.

She saw a good deal of the Austrian at Fairhaven, but she rarely invited him to the cottage, much as she enjoyed his company. He would have come gladly, she was well aware, but the last thing she could allow herself to do was give him false encouragement. Then, one evening, he came anyway, to deliver a book that she'd expressed an interest in reading. He timed his visit carefully and there was nothing for it but to ask him in to share a pre-supper drink. The book when he handed it to her was mint-new. She was delighted to have it, but embarrassed enough as well to be forthright with him.

"You're cheating, Peter. I thought you had this already, but it's straight off the press. I didn't mean you to get it specially."

"I know," he admitted with his gentle smile, "but it's a pleasure to do things for you. May I not be selfish to that extent?"

Her own smile thanked him for the kindness, but his expression had become serious and sad. There was a slight tremor in the hand holding his glass, and she had a presentiment of what was coming next.

"Anna, I'd be happy to do much more for you, but there's no need to tell me that it's hopeless; you've been so careful to discourage me – with the utmost gentleness, I hasten to say! But I just want you to know that I love you very much. That won't change, so it won't ever be too late if *you* should change."

He managed to make the little speech so lightly that their friendship wasn't fractured by embarrassment or hurt; they could go on as before, because he wouldn't allow any discomfort to creep in. She was heart-sick to disappoint him all the same, and shaken by the knowledge of her own foolishness. There couldn't be another man alive who so dearly deserved loving, and on her own account what had she to look forward to instead but the frustrated longings of a stupid, unbiddable heart.

"If I had a grain of sense it wouldn't be hopeless," she said quietly. "Why aren't feelings less stubborn, and less senseless than they are?"

His little shrug offered all the answer there was – the heart had its reasons, *nicht wahr*? "Now we'll think of other things," he suggested. "Tell me how the book is going."

She forced herself to talk about it, knowing that he meant her to follow his lead. It wasn't even the time to confront him with the problem of Denise Trotter, although she was still waiting for him to return to the subject of her ruined painting.

She was hard at work the next morning when a tap on the window announced that Harriet was waiting on the path outside. Anna opened the door about to say that her friend had smelled the coffee-break looming, but Harriet's face suggested some different reason for calling.

It was sheet-white under it's summer coating of freckles and, in the kitchen where Anna automatically led her, she ducked her head to ward off sudden faintness. She recovered herself at once and looked up, trying to smile. "Emptiness, I expect – I did eat breakfast, but lost it again soon afterwards!"

Anna quickly filled mugs with coffee, then sat down beside Harriet at the table.

"Drink some of that first, then tell me what's wrong."

She was offered a single sheet of paper – badly

crumpled as if Harriet's first intention had been to destroy it.

It was a letter, crudely written in block capitals, and the message was crude as well. Harriet ought to know, it said, that her husband, in the course of frequent visits to a certain cottage in the strand, was the lover of the disgraceful artist who lived there.

"Do you believe it?" Anna managed to ask between stiff lips.

Harriet answered with a simplicity that at least left no room for doubt. "Idiot. Of course not! I nearly tore the filthy thing up. In fact I was in two minds about even telling *you*. I *shan't* tell Robin, but in the end I decided that you ought to know. Someone's got their knife into you, Anna."

"It doesn't come as a surprise," she admitted slowly, stroking Ulysses' rough head. He'd come to sit beside her, sensing as usual when comfort was needed. "Something *is* going on, although I can't explain it or pin it down. I nearly told Peter about it the other day, but he's got problems enough at Fairhaven at the moment, and it didn't seem fair to burden him with mine when he isn't involved."

"Well I am, according to this disgusting note; so you'd better come clean."

"People here have been very kind," Anna began with difficulty. "Almost overpoweringly friendly, in fact. But several times lately I've had the feeling that women who used to smile and say good morning have begun to look the other way. I pretended to myself that I was imagining it. Then, going into the supermarket yesterday morning, a woman I didn't even recognise actually drew her skirt aside as I went in. I can't explain how shocking it was . . . I felt like a leper, transported back in time to some primitive, taboo-ridden society!" She tried to smile, to lessen the horror in Harriet's face. "If I'm doing something that upsets people, I wish I knew what it was; otherwise I shall go on doing it and make matters worse!"

Harriet leaned over to wrap warm arms about her. "It's some poor creature with a sick mind, love. There *are* such people, even here; they accumulate spleen inside themselves and have to let some of it out occasionally. Anna, don't look sad. You've been made a target because you're new here – you look different from the rest of us, more exotic and rare. We'll burn this beastly thing now and forget it. I forbid you to think that anyone but a poor, demented crackpot couldn't want you here."

She planted a kiss on Anna's cheek, smiled reassuringly, and left with the reminder that a weekend visit would be expected as usual. Alone again, Anna pretended to go back to work, but it was a wasted effort. She knew now that she *hadn't* imagined the web of hostility that seemed to be closing around her, and she could put no faith in Harriet's comforting idea that it was ill-will directed at a newcomer. Someone other than a disturbed teenager disliked her enough to want to drive her away, and the poison of distrust could be made to spread easily in a small, compact world that still clung to the habits and standards of the past. With the usual perversity of life it seemed that she'd learned to love a place that refused to love her.

A sleepless night followed the unproductive day, and she was thankful to get up and brew a restoring cup of coffee. The kitchen clock said ten past six – hours too early for a caller, even though she thought she heard the sound of a light tap at the front door. But Ulysses' cocked head confirmed that he'd caught the noise too.

"A seagull reminding us he's hungry?" she suggested to him. But when she opened the door, expecting to find no one there, Hugo stood propping up the wall as if it was the only thing that kept him upright. His face looked grey with exhaustion, and in her sudden certainty that some kind of need had brought him there it didn't occur to her to send him away, or even to remember the terms of their last unfriendly conversation.

"I thought I'd risk a little knock, Anna," he murmured quietly. "Not enough to wake you if you weren't up and about already."

She said nothing at all until he'd followed her into the kitchen and slumped into a chair at the table.

"Coffee?" she asked abruptly.

"Please . . . It's been a longish night. My old friend, Ben Trevithian, finally died a little while ago."

She ladled sugar into a mug of coffee and put it in front of him before answering.

"He won't have been sorry to die, Hugo. He was the most contented man I've ever met. No one else's good fortune rankled; he didn't even covet their good health. Ben's conviction was that he'd had his turn and made the most of it. 'No dishonour and no regrets' – that's what he said to

137

me once with proper pride." She wanted to weep
for the sadness in Hugo's face, but could only allow
herself to sound sharp instead. "I suppose you're
blaming yourself because you couldn't keep him
alive a little longer? Every failure has to be your
own."

He simply shook his head. "I felt that in Africa
certainly, every time I had to watch a young child
die. It doesn't apply in Ben's case; the loss is only
mine because he was a friend." He stared at Anna,
sitting opposite him at the table, Ulysses inevitably
close by her side. "Your visits gave Ben enormous
pleasure – a lovely present to finish up with was how
he described them to me."

She was suddenly tempted to pour out the truth –
that even dear, kind Ben might have shut the door
in her face if he'd still been on visiting terms with
his neighbours and been told of her new reputation.
Hugo himself ought to be warned to stay away from
her in future. But not just yet, she decided helplessly.
Whatever some damned, poisonous puritan would
make of it, she must now give Hugo any comfort
that she could. The long night had stripped him of
the guard he normally kept upon himself, and only
later would it seem possible to wonder why he hadn't
gone to Judith Jackson instead.

"If you'll share Ulysses' early morning stroll I'll
have breakfast ready when you get back," she suggested.

He looked from her to the dog now watching him
expectantly. "Does he understand every mortal thing
you say?"

"Just about," she agreed. "It makes conversation very easy!"

Hugo smiled but simply followed Ulysses to the door without commenting.

By the time they reappeared the kitchen smelled warmly inviting after the freshness of the air outside. She brought bacon and eggs, toast and more coffee to the table, and invited him calmly to sit and eat. She was, he realised, as far removed from his first perception of her as any woman could be. Though obviously beautiful and clearly talented, the rest of his glib assessment had been ludicrously wide of the mark. Sophisticated, selfish and self-pitying, he'd rashly thought, but others here, more clear-sighted than himself, had seen the truth about her. Only Judith had completely resisted the charm of Anna Carteret . . . Judith! Even the sound of her name in his mind was weighed down by guilt and sadness.

It wasn't *her* fault, their failure to create that mixture of excitement and contentment and delight that true lovers knew. She'd offered herself already in terms that couldn't be refused, but sex – however feverishly sampled – wasn't love; the wonderment of feeling complete together hadn't happened at all, and the blame for it was entirely his.

In the quiet peacefulness of Anna's kitchen he fully understood the magnitude of the mistake he'd made, but it was a mistake that he would have to learn to live with. To another woman he might have been able to explain; to Judith, cruelly deprived of happiness once before and only too eager to be offered the chance of it again with him, it was impossible; the

139

mere thought of walking away made him wince with shame.

That agonising communion with himself had been necessary, but he refused to consider why it should have seemed so necessary *now*. Instead, he looked at the girl sitting quietly opposite him and managed a less than convincing smile.

"You'll make someone a perfect wife – no chatter at the breakfast-table!"

"I don't mind a little conversation myself," she pointed out, "but you looked too deep in thought to be interrupted." Too troubled, she might more truthfully have said, if she hadn't been certain that it was a trouble she could do nothing about. She remembered what Peter Hubner had admitted – Hugo longed for the day when he could go back to Africa, but perhaps already knew in his heart how hopeless the longing was. Her dark eyes were so full of pity that he was afraid for a moment that she knew of the snare he was caught in. With a huge effort he managed a more natural tone of voice.

"Mercifully for doctors, there often comes a moment after a sleepless night when the mind functions with unusual clarity. That happened to me just now, and I was seeing the future steadily and seeing it whole, as they say! But I'm sorry if I was rude enough to ignore the very kind provider of a delicious breakfast in the process."

She hovered on the edge of saying that there were more than enough people nearer at hand needing his care without going to Africa to find them; but pointing out the obvious was a futile occupation at the best of times. Instead, she offered him the lovely smile that he was less familiar with than his friends were.

"The cook took no umbrage, having great thoughts of her own to deal with!"

He nodded, hesitated over what he might have said next, and then abruptly got to his feet. "I must be off now. I'll let you know the time of Ben's funeral."

A moment later he'd let himself out of the cottage and she and Ulysses were alone again. She stacked plates in the sink, and went on doing it blindly despite the tears that began to trickle down her cheeks. It was Ben she was weeping for, she told the dog who pattered back and forth beside her; that was all that ailed her – grief for a friend who'd died – and there was nothing wrong in giving way to that.

Twelve

J udith was trained to observe people, but as a nurse is trained – equating the alterations she saw only with physical causes. She despised Peter Hubner's insistence on the importance of states of mind as well. In Hugo's case, though, she was forced to concede something to the Hubner theory. There, mind, not body, was the obstacle she was up against. Outwardly he was the same man: courteous, kind and apparently appreciative; he even occasionally made a brave show of still wanting her, but now she sensed the effort it required. Ben's death had something to do with it – a reminder of mortality and decay was bound to dull the appetite for a while. But it didn't explain why she had the impression, faint but unmistakable, that she was sharing life now with a ghost.

Marriage, rather than their present relationship, would help; Hugo was a stiff-necked Highlander, after all. But whenever she led the conversation round to a date for their wedding it seemed to end with nothing decided on. That wasn't ideal – he shouldn't have been in so little of a hurry to claim a wife; but Judith didn't expect too much. The proposal had at least come when she'd almost despaired of getting it, and she was safe now. Hugo wasn't the man to let a woman down.

She remained more patient than he deserved, and thought he was aware of the fact. Things were slowly improving again, she reckoned, when he made a casual reference one day to a letter from Simon Redfern.

"Simon writes to ask whether he can come as usual – next weekend, he suggests." It wasn't a question as such; Hugo assumed that she would relish the idea as much as he did. Instead, he was astonished by the fierceness of her reply.

"He battens on you – like a lot of other people. Let him find someone else to give him a free holiday for a change."

She meant it, he realised with deep dismay and puzzlement, but even so he tried to reason with her. "Simon's *our* friend. He loves it here, and rightly takes it for granted that he's always welcome to come." Judith's expression didn't soften and he was provoked into adding something he'd intended not to mention. "By the way, Simon didn't consult me about the wisdom of letting Neville know where Anna was, so I suppose he must have asked you?"

She gave a little shrug. "Yes, he asked – she was supposed to be pining for the man, and I was doing her a good turn, I thought. He certainly looked very much at home when we called."

Hugo knew that he couldn't fairly quarrel with that; it had been his own disagreeable impression. But he remembered Judith's strange insistence that evening that they should visit Anna; now, for the first time, it occurred to him to wonder whether she could possibly have known when Neville was going to be there. The suspicion made him speak with a sharpness he'd never offered her before.

"On this occasion your advice was ill-judged, I think."

"Because the fascinating Miss Carteret had got bored with him by the time he arrived? I suppose she finds it more exciting now to add a few local scalps to her belt." Goaded by Hugo's expression, she was provoked into rashness. "Everyone seems to be besotted with her here – Michael Harding and Robin Grayson to name but two, judging by the amount of time they spend at her cottage."

"Unpardonable, Judith," said Hugo, now white with anger. "You know as well as I do why Michael goes there – to work with Anna on their book; and at the moment Robin is helping her to arrange the children's painting exhibition. I beg you *not* to voice that opinion to anyone else."

The distaste in his face shocked her first into silence, and then into an apology.

"Sorry, Hugo . . . I didn't mean to sound such a bitch! I'm just tired and irritable, and wishing that instead of having Simon here we could get away ourselves for a while. It would still be warm in the south of France . . . couldn't we go – just for a week or two?"

She looked beautifully contrite, and Hugo found himself ashamedly hoping that she never heard of his own call at the cottage after Ben died. He wished with all his heart that he could love her as she deserved, but it was the behaviour of a fool to hope that love would come with waiting; he must manage without it somehow.

"Let Simon have his holiday," he suggested gently. "The poor chap probably needs it badly. After that we'll combine a holiday of our own and a honeymoon anywhere you like."

The smell of burning boats was strong in his nostrils, but the decision came almost as a relief, and Judith's radiant smile told him how unpardonably long he'd been in grasping the nettle of a marriage that must sooner rather than later take place. She kissed him more lingeringly than usual, but resisted the temptation to reopen a subject occasionally aired before. Her firm intention was *not* to spend the rest of her life on St Mary's, or to have much more of Hugo's wealth frittered away on the derelict children he brought there. She considered that both of them had toiled long enough among the world's unfortunates; it was time to think of themselves. But the blank dismay on Hugo's face when she'd hinted at some influential appointment in London had warned her that it was an idea she must make slow haste with. Their wedding was the first hurdle to get over safely. Simon's visit was ill-timed and irritating, but there was no reason to feel nervous about it, and she'd been stupid to seem hostile. She'd lost a little ground with Hugo as a result, and must tread more carefully in future.

Morag might win no prizes as an innovative cook, but it was a matter of pride with her to keep the doctor's house in a state of shining orderliness. If a guest was expected, his room was ready for him days before there was the slightest chance of his arriving, and knowing this, Simon Redfern didn't hesitate about walking off the *Scillonian* a full twenty-four hours before he was due to reach St Mary's.

It happened to be Anna, walking back along the quay with Ulysses one lunchtime, who was the first to see him. She had a moment's difficulty in identifying the man who'd seen her in some of her most unhappy moments, but when he hesitated in front of her she remembered that he'd talked about his own annual visit to the Scillies. Six months ago she would probably have turned and hurried in the opposite direction, but now she stopped and held out her hand.

"You don't seem to recognise me, I'm delighted to say!" she pointed out cheerfully. "Anna Carteret – much less sickly than when you saw me last."

Simon examined her with pleasure, thinking that the contrast was astonishing between this warmly-smiling girl and the sad, hostile creature whose departure from St Martha's had so worried him. "Not so much 'less sickly' as transformed," he said with a delighted grin. "I didn't realise that you intended to settle down here, but Scillies life clearly suits you."

They walked along together, both having tacitly decided to start their acquaintance again, with no awkward references to the past. Simon would have liked to ask about the unhappy man who'd come to see him in London, but he could see danger in the subject and sensibly left it alone. For the same reason Anna overlooked his interference in her life, and they parted amicably at the door of her cottage.

He made his peace with Morag for arriving before he was expected, and re-established himself in the house he looked upon as his second home. His bag was unpacked and he was stretched out on the terrace, gratefully enjoying the evening sunshine, when Hugo returned from an afternoon at Fairhaven.

Their friendship went back even to pre-student days and the affection between them was strong and true. Tired himself, and overdue for a rest, Simon was shocked by the thinness of Hugo's face; no doubt the gauntness was due to the fever that had brought him home, but it looked as if it would now be his own thankless task to convince a stubborn man of the madness of trying to get back to Africa again – it would be thoroughly unfair to Judith as well. They talked medical shop for a while, and then Simon brought the conversation round to personal affairs.

"When's the wedding to be?" he wanted to know. "You can't get married without a best man, and I'll need at least a few days' notice if I'm to wangle another quick trip down here."

"Not just yet . . . Some time in October, I think," Hugo answered, trying not to wince at his own heartiness. "I hope you'll come, of course, but you won't have to take any arduous part – Judith seems to favour a registry office affair."

He was staring out over the sunlit water as he spoke, and Simon let a little silence fall between them before he ventured on a more difficult question. "Anything wrong, Hugo? You look rotten if you don't mind an old friend saying so."

Their glasses needed refilling, and Hugo took his time about the small task while he found an answer that would serve. "End-of-summer blues, I expect . . . Nothing a holiday won't cure."

"What about Judith . . . ? Is she all right?"

"Yes, but much more deserving of a break, and she's not as content with the islands as I am. A hint emerges now and then that she'd like a less remote setting for married life. I'm not quite sure how we're going to resolve that problem, but it will work itself out as soon as I get the OK to start back in harness again." It reasonably explained the air of strain he knew that his friend had detected, but he threw in a confident smile for good measure, and Simon was kind enough to let the subject drop. Instead, it was safer to talk of local matters, and he was reminded of his meeting with Anna on the quay.

"I scarcely recognised her," he said thoughtfully. "Not because she'd grown beautiful – it was obvious that she would be when she didn't look ill and unhappy – but I seemed to be talking to a different girl. Even battered as she was in hospital, she still squared up to me; this afternoon, though, she was friendly and serene – quite able to cope with adversity now, I should think, if it arose again."

Hugo stared at the contents of his glass. "You seem to have noticed quite a lot during a brief walk together."

"Professional observation," Simon said blandly. "Does the fellow who came to see me have anything to do with her present well-being?"

"It seems not," came the almost too-casual reply.

"Neville did pay her a visit, but he didn't stay. The real explanation for the change in her seems to be that she's found friends here. She's also busy as well – collaborating with Michael Harding on a book about the islands. By Michael's account of it, it's going to be beautiful."

His voice expressed only a detached interest in the subject of Anna Carteret and, for once finding conversation with Hugo difficult, Simon struggled on. "I gather she knows the Graysons very well? She said she's become a sort of adopted aunt to the children."

"Well, what she probably *didn't* say is that she saved Colin's life when a bit of Garrison collapsed underneath him one wild day."

"No," Simon agreed quietly. "She didn't mention that."

Judith came to share their supper that evening, and he watched her with a mixture of curiosity and concern. But in the end he was left simply admiring her. She was warm and affable towards himself, but made it clear that her dependence and delight was all in Hugo. Her behaviour, in fact, was perfect and he found himself blaming his friend for the slight constraint he couldn't help detecting in the atmosphere. It wasn't like Hugo to let a hankering for what he couldn't have make him irritable.

But as the slow, lazy days went by, Simon watched and wondered and gradually understood – something was eating the heart out of his friend, and it wasn't simply inactivity or frustration.

Nevertheless, there was to be a party, Hugo insisted. He had a guest to entertain, and mountainous debts of hospitality to repay. As a sensible host he intended to settle both accounts with one exhausting but successful event. With Judith busy at Fairhaven during the day, and Morag implored *not* to let party food disrupt her rota, it was left to Harriet Grayson to take charge of the kitchen. With Alice's and Morag's help, she was to contrive an elegant buffet supper, while Simon was given the task of providing adequate supplies of wine. There was nothing left for Hugo to do but wander in from an afternoon spent helping out at the hospital to inspect the efforts of his exhausted helpers.

"Delegate," he murmured happily, dodging a roll aimed at him by Simon. "It's well known to be the secret of a stress-free life!"

He seemed at last to have recovered some of his old gaiety, and he greeted Judith's arrival in advance of the other guests with a show of pleasure that for once looked natural and unstrained. She had deserted her usual blue for a dress of rose-coloured silk, and the glowing colour suited her. Looking younger than her workaday self, she was even more lovely, and a note of teasing ownership established her position without overstressing it. Altogether things were going so well that Simon was on the verge of deciding that he'd imagined Hugo's unhappiness. There was nothing to worry about after all, and when the time came an old friend would have only to pilot the couple through the wedding ceremony.

He was enjoying the party – arguing with James Ferguson as to whether doctors or vets were the more put upon by their customers – when he saw Anna Carteret arrive. She hesitated for a moment in the doorway of the crowded room as if looking for a friend, and there was time to register the picture she made; simple tunic of cream linen, fragile green sandals on her bare feet. Simon felt suddenly sorry for all the other women in the room – the poor things had probably laboured long to achieve much less effect.

Still watching, he became aware of the precise moment when Hugo caught sight of her, and his own heart missed a beat at the unguarded expression on his friend's face. It was only the briefest flash of time before the mask of smiling ease was back in place, but there wasn't any doubt about it – naked longing and pain had momentarily taken possession of Hugo's face and left him defenceless. Simon looked away and found himself staring at Judith instead. She'd seen what he'd seen – he knew it, and felt deeply sorry for her. But from then on she didn't leave Hugo's side and he couldn't blame her for it; it was time to behave as if she were already the mistress of the house.

Warned by the knife-flick of Judith's smile that she would have done better to stay at home, Anna took refuge with people as far removed from her hosts as possible. She had done what seemed called for – put in an appearance that had cost her something in courage; now, as soon as possible, she would go, and leave Judith triumphantly in possession. Choosing a moment when Hugo had left the room, she began to edge her way out, but Judith appeared beside her, eyes glinting like jewels, with malice instead of reflected light.

"Not going already, surely," she suggested sweetly. "You've only just arrived."

"Work calls, I'm afraid," Anna explained with a brave attempt at lightness.

"Ah yes, work . . . More collaboration, no doubt! I suppose we shall see someone else slipping out as well in a moment or two."

Delivered with deliberate intent in Judith's clear voice, the words produced a hush around them – they might have been meant in fun, but not when every separate syllable dripped venom. Anna looked from Judith's smiling face to Peter Hubner, willing him not to intervene on her behalf and make matters worse than they already were.

"No one else need leave on my account," she managed to say calmly.

"Come now, Anna. You mustn't be so modest. We all know that the bewitching artist from London has all our menfolk in thrall!"

If there'd been any doubt before, there was none now; this wasn't a game, but open war. Anna's face had gone sheet-white under its tan, but she trampled on the memory of the letter Harriet had received. It was a coincidence that Judith's jibe had been couched in rather similar terms. She refused to believe that the woman Hugo was going to marry could be capable of such spite. It was only that the label of a bohemian harlot had somehow got generally attached to her. Feeling sick, she managed to smile at her tormentor.

"Mistaken identity," she murmured. "My name's not Circe! Now, I'll say goodnight."

She walked away from the house, thinking that

152

she'd set foot in it for the second and last time. That was better than going over the scene she'd just left, or wondering whether she would be able to stay on the island long enough to complete the book with Michael. Judith only seemed to share an idea that was generally held. Perhaps there *was* some alien aura that artists inevitably dragged around with them which made them unacceptable to their normally kind and tolerant neighbours. Common sense instructed her not to be stampeded into running away – she had responsibilities now – Ulysses, and a cottage of her own. But she couldn't live perpetually in an atmosphere of distrust and disapproval; nor, above all, could she bear for that recent scene with Judith ever to be repeated. Perhaps, in the end, she and Ulysses would have to start wandering again. It was as far as thought would take her for the moment because the pain of this fresh exile seemed likely to be almost more than she could bear.

At the party she'd left behind, Judith continued to smile and chatter brightly, and gradually the rent she'd torn in the evening's gaiety was uneasily repaired. Hugo seemed not to notice Anna's departure, and no one, least of all Simon, felt inclined to explain why she was no longer there. Judith at least was satisfied, certain that the threat Anna Carteret had seemed to present had now disappeared. It was her philosophy of life, honed by hardship and experience, to get what she wanted by fighting for it. Relying on an opponent to walk away from the field was not only feeble, in Judith's view, but also stupid as well. She wanted the settled, secure life that Hugo would provide; and at the age of thirty-five she was prepared to forego what she might also have insisted on a year or two ago. He didn't value her in the way she deserved; might, she suspected, be profoundly relieved if she were silly enough to allow him to slip away. But although William's death wasn't something for which he could be rightly blamed, he felt responsible and he'd slaughter his own hope of happiness or peace of mind not to let her down. She almost despised him for it in a way; it wasn't how she'd fought herself free of a miserable childhood. But people like Hugo, and no doubt Anna Carteret as well, didn't know anything of that; they'd had an easier life. They deserved to be beaten by fighters like herself.

Thirteen

Looking back afterwards, it seemed to Anna that the night of Hugo's party marked a turning-point in all their lives. Even if it produced nothing startlingly dramatic at the time, the events that followed began to gather the kind of momentum that couldn't be halted, much less put into reverse.

The next afternoon Michael came as usual to bring a week's work for her to see, but didn't stay to share her supper; Elizabeth was pinned to her chair with a badly-sprained ankle and he was needed at home. When he let himself out of the cottage, therefore, it was still light enough for him and the woman passing by to be able to recognise each other. Michael's nod was no more than polite – he didn't like Mrs Hughes-Watson. She wasn't an islander, and although he normally welcomed newcomers to the community, this was the sort of affluent and pushy widow from the mainland that he reckoned they could well have done without. She'd mistaken Elizabeth soon after her arrival for an insignificant piano teacher who didn't count in the social scheme of things. His sister had thought it mildly funny, but Michael judged the woman to be insensitive and a fool.

Now, even as he framed a brief 'good evening' it became apparent that it wouldn't be necessary. Mrs Hughes-Watson was eyeing him with what looked remarkably like disgust – disgust laced with a kind of avid curiosity whose meaning was unmistakeable. He walked home in a state of uncharacteristic rage, and went straight to the sideboard in the dining-room to pour himself a glass of whisky.

"Are you going to tell me what's upset you, or sit there glowering for the rest of the evening?" Elizabeth asked eventually.

"I'm still trying to pretend that I misinterpreted what happened," he grunted.

"And I'm still trying to discover what *did* happen," she pointed out.

"I met that Hughes-Watson woman as I was leaving Anna's cottage. Even now I can scarcely believe it, but she managed to make me feel like a lout furtively creeping out of a brothel!" He stared at Elizabeth and she wasn't inclined to smile, seeing the extent of his distress. "I *didn't* imagine it – that damned woman actually sniffed as she went past. I should have done something about tackling her there and then, but she scuttled away as if I'd got the plague, and I was too angry to think straight in any case."

"What *can* you do about it?"

"I don't know. . . . What we all do, I suppose – take the problem to Hugo."

Elizabeth hesitated for a moment. "No, don't do that. Mrs Hughes-Watson has become a bosom friend of Judith's." She stopped again, appalled by the enormity of what needed saying. "Michael, I hope

I'm wrong, but I can't help feeling that the two of them are involved in a whispering campaign that is going on against us."

"You mean there's more to it than just the little brush I had this afternoon?"

"Nothing quite definite enough to pin down, but I'd swear that there's been a change in the atmosphere. You know how friendly the place usually is, but several times lately I've seen Anna ignored in the shops. It could have been accidental, of course, but I don't think so. I go charging up to her, and we pretend not to have noticed, but I know from her face that she has."

"Well, something's got to be done. She'll have to come here in future, but I can't change the arrangements without explaining why. We shall have to tell her about this afternoon, and try – though God knows how – to make it sound daft enough to be funny."

A fine afternoon had given Simon Redfern the excuse to borrow Hugo's boat and invite Peter Hubner to go fishing. But although they chugged to a bay that looked promising, he was in no hurry to set up his rod. He suddenly plunged into conversation instead.

"Do you know what possessed Hugo to propose to Judith? It's the strangest engagement I've ever come across. He's not in love with her – I'm certain of that; and there are times when I'm not even sure he likes her very much."

Hubner gave his usual shrug. "The reason's simple enough. Judith was ready to sleep with him, but Hugo wanted a wife. I doubt if she's the wife he wanted, but he seemed to have the idea that he could make it work. It's only the second stupid thing I've known him do." He thought over what he'd just said, and feared that it sounded disloyal. "There's also the fact, of course, that he feels responsible for her. He still blames himself for letting William go to Africa with him."

Simon stared out across the seascape of islands and blue water; then when his companion thought the conversation was over he began to speak again. "He couldn't have *stopped* William going. The poor chap was hell-bent on getting away from Judith. She tricked him into marrying her, but he accidentally found out about it and never forgave her."

"*How* tricked?" Hubner asked. "Did he say?"

"Yes . . . I don't think he meant to, but he'd been drinking heavily one night before he went away and suddenly it all came flooding out. There'd been a poison pen letter about them – damaging to him, and even more so to Judith; you know what fiendishly gossipy places hospitals are. Afterwards he discovered quite by chance that, far from the letter being anonymous, Judith had written it herself – to force his hand a bit, I suppose." He stared at the Austrian's pale face. "Do you want to go back? Feeling seasick, Peter?"

"Just sick," Hubner answered with difficulty. "This is the woman we have at Fairhaven, looking after disturbed adolescents."

Simon's own expression was equally wretched now. "Perhaps I should have told you when I knew Hugo was bringing Judith here. But I decided that she'd made a mistake and paid for it. She needed help, and I knew there wasn't any doubt about her professional competence. In the end I reckoned that what William had told me could die with him. But I'm afraid it never crossed my mind that Hugo would finish up marrying her. He hasn't looked at another woman since Kirstie died."

"He's begun to look at one now," Hubner said sombrely, "and Judith is aware of the fact that even if she's content with their relationship, Hugo is not." Then he lifted his hand in a gesture that pushed the matter aside. "We came out to go fishing, my friend. Hadn't we better have something to show for an afternoon's work?"

They went back eventually with some bass that Morag might consider worth cooking, and it wasn't until they parted company on the jetty that Hubner suddenly reverted to the subject of Hugo.

"I don't think he will get much joy from his marriage, but it will certainly take place, because Judith will hold him to it. He wouldn't, in any case, be the man to back out. She's too intelligent not to know the value of what she's got, and we must pray that good fortune makes her a good wife."

Simon's nod agreed, and there the matter rested.

But back at Fairhaven Hubner found the very woman they'd been discussing waiting for him in his study. It was the time when she should have been supervising the younger children's supper and bath routine, and he hoped that the unexpectedness of her visit would account for the momentary hesitation she probably noticed in him. He had to work with her and must forget what Simon had told him, but it required more of an effort, he now found, than he'd expected.

"Good evening, Judith. You look worried. How can I help?"

"It's Denise," she said abruptly. "The child missed lunch and hasn't been seen since. I've tried to search the building without alarming anyone else, but there's still no sign of her and I'm getting anxious."

"Are you thinking that it's some kind of game? To cause us all alarm?"

"I don't *know*," Judith snapped. "She hasn't done anything like this before."

"But you *are* in her confidence at the moment," he pointed out quietly. "In fact you've made more of a protégée of her than I've thought wise, but you know that already."

The reproof made Judith bridle a little. "She's been unhappy lately. That's all I can tell you."

The Austrian's face, normally so gentle in its expression, seemed to have become that of a stern stranger. "It's not quite all I must tell *you*. Denise is *more* unstable now than when she arrived here, not less. You insisted on making a friend of her, and then forgot about her when Hugo began to take up more of your spare time. Denise can't handle that sort of rejection."

"I took an interest in her," Judith shouted. "It was *you* she felt rejected by. It's no wonder she threw paint at Anna Carteret's stupid drawing."

Peter Hubner stared at the woman in front of him, wondering if she'd been irresponsible enough to encourage the damage. After a moment he managed to speak calmly. "You're an excellent nurse and administrator, but you're not trained in the sort of problem Denise represents."

"Problem! Case history!" Judith bit out the words with scorn. "*I* was trying to treat her as a human being."

"With this result, it seems. I must insist that you leave her to me in future, Judith; otherwise I shall be forced to tell Hugo that you're dangerously exceeding your duties here. Now, though, we must find her and end the game before it gets out of hand."

Colour rushed into her face, but he didn't wait for her to answer and walked out of the room.

With the help of the rest of the staff they combed Fairhaven inside and out, until there was no possibility left that she could be there. It was now past seven, and the early October dusk was falling. Six hours had passed since anyone could remember seeing her – in an institution where a regularly fixed routine was part and parcel of the children's return to normal life. If she'd taken refuge in a café or pub, Hubner knew that he'd have been informed by now; they had reached the point where it was likely to be a game no longer and her disappearance must be notified. He rang Hugo first, then the Police Station, and the two of them met there.

With Simon, Michael Harding, Robin Grayson and a dozen other helpers organised by the police sergeant, they spent a wearying and wasted night hunting for a small, sulky, unhappy adolescent. The night wasn't cold, and she could survive out in the open well enough, but Hubner was haunted by the knowledge that by now she was probably very frightened. His worse fear was shared by all of them – there were a dozen places around the island where she could have fallen into the sea.

In the half-light of a grey, depressing dawn they trudged back to Fairhaven, too tired for the moment to plan where to search next. The police had now extended the hunt to the mainland, in case Denise had managed to get herself on board the steamer during the afternoon and arrived in Penzance. For the moment there was nothing more to do but drink the coffee Judith had waiting for them, and snatch a brief rest while others took over. Hugo sent the team home to bed, insisting that he would wait by the telephone. His own face was shadowed with weariness, but when he issued instructions they knew better than to argue with him.

The search so far had covered all the obvious places and most of the unobvious ones as well, but no one had thought of looking in the outhouse at the bottom of Anna's courtyard garden. This was where Denise still cowered, penned there by an enormous, terrifying hound whose existence she hadn't known about.

It had been a simple matter to get into the cottage Judith had once pointed out to her. Too simple, really. The back gate had been left unlocked, and some of the excitement of the illicit visit had already drained away. She'd hoped to find the cottage empty but, spying Anna, had settled down in the shed to wait for darkness to fall. It seemed a terribly long time before Anna came out to bolt the gate, and the light in the upstairs room finally went out.

Feeling suddenly much less confident in the darkness, Denise had left the now-familiar shed, and crept over to the open kitchen window, clutching the small knife she'd remembered to bring. Then terror struck, in the form of a dark shape baying at her from the other side of the glass. The noise itself was enough to wake the dead, and Denise fled back to her refuge again, sick and trembling with fear. A light shone briefly downstairs, as if someone had come to investigate; then darkness again, silence, and that great creature still lying in wait.

She sat on the dusty floor, and finally sobbed herself into a doze that lasted until it grew light. With the dawn came a small return of courage. The idea of getting into the house had long since been abandoned, but she thought she might reach the gate without being seen – if she just timed it right. She was halfway there when Anna opened the kitchen door for Ulysses to take his early morning stroll round the garden. His warning bark, deep-throated now that he was almost fully grown, transfixed a girl whose life hadn't so far included a dog of any size. Then, as he leapt towards her, she gave a scream of pure terror. Running from the kitchen, Anna saw the knife in her hand and shouted desperately at Ulysses to keep away. But a moment later she realised that her dog was in no danger – the girl was rigid with fear, incapable of moving.

"He won't hurt you," she said unevenly. "He only sounds fierce."

She commanded Ulysses to sit down, then reached

over and removed the knife from Denise's hand. The girl's fingers were ice-cold and she gave no resistance when she was led inside the house.

"If you've been there all night I suggest you get into a hot bath; we'll have breakfast when you've thawed out again," Anna said casually. Her guest might just have spent a normal night on the premises, her voice seemed to imply, but she hadn't missed the fear and misery in the girl's rigid face, and could only guess at the anxiety Peter Hubner must be feeling. She waited until Denise was safely occupied in the bathroom and then telephoned Fairhaven.

"Peter . . . ? No, it's Hugo, surely. I've just found Denise Trotter in my garden. She seems to have spent the night. I suppose you knew she was missing?"

"We've spent the entire night looking for her," Hugo said briefly. "Is she all right?"

"Cold, frightened and hungry. Nothing worse than that, I think."

"Thank God! I'll come over straightaway."

"No, don't. Well, what I mean is, why not leave it for an hour or so? She was in sore need of a hot bath, and after that I was intending to feed her. I have the feeling that she's desperate to talk, and since she must have had a reason for coming here, it might help to find out what it was."

"Perhaps," he agreed reluctantly. "Provided you can manage on your own. She's not always very obedient, Anna – are you sure you don't want help?"

"Let me try, please. She brought a knife with her, but I'm pretty certain that it wasn't meant for me."

*   *   *

With the conversation over, Hugo looked thankfully at Judith sitting beside him. "You'll have gathered that she's safe. No further away than Anna's garden shed, where she spent an uncomfortable night."

"You're not going to leave her there, surely?"

"For the moment. Anna's idea is that a quiet meal together might help." He studied Judith's face for a moment. "I get the impression that you don't think so. Why not?"

Judith gave a little shrug, then made up her mind; the risk, though dangerous, was unavoidable now. "You'll hate me for saying this, Hugo, but you did ask for my opinion. I'm sure Denise had a purpose in going to Anna Carteret's cottage, melodramatic and stupid though it might seem to us. Peter Hubner spent a lot of time with the child to begin with – too much in my opinion – and now she feels neglected. Denise's philosophy is the one that life has taught her – recognise your enemy and then go for her. She sees Anna, I'm afraid, as the woman who now attracts a man she looked upon as her own property."

Silence filled the room, but it was better than the furious outburst she expected. Encouraged, she decided to go on in the same quiet voice as before. "I know you value Peter Hubner; he's a friend, and you count loyalty to friends as an important virtue. Well, so do I. But I'm bound to say, Hugo, that I don't think you found the right man to be in charge at Fairhaven. His mistake with Denise hasn't ended in disaster, but we might not be so lucky another time. It does us no good to have him under the thumb of a woman who is becoming something of a public scandal."

She saw the storm gathering in Hugo's face, but held up her hand, insisting that he listen. "My dear, you and I come from sophisticated regions; we discount behaviour that strikes the people here as something they can't accept. Hugh Town's too small a place for it not to be known that Anna keeps open house – Neville, Peter, Michael, Robin . . . There may be others as well for all I know." She spoke without heat or rancour, and had the feeling that for once he was listening to her. It was surely the moment to risk a little more. "Fairhaven is becoming too much of a headache, Hugo. Let's close it down, please. Start again together somewhere else."

She thought the past night had left him discouraged, and almost uncertain for once; now, it was safe to sound strong for both of them. She felt as sure-footed as a cat picking its way among hazards. "Darling, give up the dream of going back to Africa. We *can* do important work, you and I – but not here in remote, tedious little Hugh Town!"

He didn't answer for a moment, remembering with painful vividness what he'd once said foolishly to Anna; far from helping him to think clearly, the sleepless night had left only a sense of muddle and mistakenness behind. Judith's argument was beginning to sound right. She was at her best when she was working, and striving together in the world they shared would give them their best chance of happiness.

He stood up abruptly, but his faint smile seemed

to express gratitude. "We'll have to think about it. Right now, I'm not in my best thinking mode!"

"What *are* you going to do?" she asked.

"First borrow a razor and give myself a much-needed shave. After that I'll go and collect Denise, and then sleep on our problems."

She watched him walk out of the room, feeling pleased with herself. Beset by dangers she might be, but there was excitement in keeping her head and picking her way through the minefield. Much as he'd wanted to deny what she'd said, he was too honest a man not to see truth when it was under his nose. It had been a risk to attack Anna and Hubner, but attack was the best method of defence – all the military manuals said so.

At the cottage Anna put toast and scrambled eggs in front of Denise, and let her demolish them in peace; it was the sort of conventional food she would probably refuse as a rule, but she was hungry now, and in her own inarticulate way too chastened to be difficult. For the moment at least, belligerence had deserted her.

Finally Anna embarked on the subject that lay uneasily between them. "You must have had an uncomfortable night, so I assume that you had a good reason for coming."

Denise considered the friendly question, examining it for the traps it almost certainly contained. Instinct told her that it would be safer to say nothing at all, but she couldn't pass up the opportunity to talk about herself . . . have someone's close attention fastened on her as this woman's certainly was.

167

"I was going to spoil all your paintings," she admitted with a kind of sullen pride.

"Why? Don't you like them?" Anna asked reasonably.

"I was sick of hearing about them from the others." Even to Denise it didn't sound much of an explanation, and it had an air of anticlimax that didn't do her justice. "I was sick of hearing about *you*, too," she insisted. "You steal people. Judith says so."

"Do you only believe what Judith tells you?"

"I know it's true. Dr Hubner liked me a lot before you came – I could tell. A girl can always tell that about men." She stared at Anna for a moment. "Well, *you* might not be able to, but I can."

"Go on," said her hostess, ignoring this thrust.

Denise looked miserable again. "Now he doesn't notice me unless he has to, but Judith says you're not satisfied with just *him*; you want to pinch her property too. I reckoned *she'd* be pleased with me if I got rid of you, and start being friends with me again."

Anna heard the sudden quiver of desolation in her voice, and understood what must have seemed to be a saga of betrayals. "You hoped I'd take the hint and leave, I suppose," she suggested quietly.

Denise nodded, still staring with distrust at Ulysses. "I had it all worked out, but that great beast there went and spoilt it all." Her voice broke suddenly at the memory of the dog leaping at her out in the courtyard, and Anna felt only pity for a child's muddled unhappiness, and rage at the way she'd been manipulated.

"Listen, please, and try to believe *me* as well as

168

Judith," she suggested. "Dr Hubner's friendship for me or anyone else doesn't alter in the slightest his care and concern for you. But he has many others in his charge as well, and in any case doctors are forbidden to get too involved with the people they're looking after. It's something called the Hippocratic Oath that they all have to swear to observe. Break it and they're fired. You can look it up if you don't want to believe me."

Denise mulled this over in silence for a moment, then grudgingly conceded a point. "I didn't know . . . Judith didn't say anything about that. I just thought he'd . . . he'd decided not to . . . to bother with me any more." She stared at her coffee-cup, afraid that if she went on trying to explain she'd burst into tears; tears were reckoned soft and silly where she'd come from.

Anna saw her struggle, and decided that it was the moment for a confession of her own. "*I* was in a mess when I came here. My life had rather fallen apart and I had no idea what I was going to do next. But the islands turned out to be exactly what I needed, and I'd begun to hope very much that I could always stay. I'm not sure that's possible any longer; but whether I go or stay, I shall do nothing to hurt your friendship with Dr Hubner, nor Judith's relationship with Dr McKay. You must believe that, because it's the truth."

She said it with all the calm conviction she could muster, and at last saw Denise nod her head. But there was one final problem she felt obliged to tackle. "Now, before you go you have to make friends with Ulysses. You've only to hold out your hand, and let him sniff it; that way he'll recognise you as a friend and offer you his paw."

It required almost more courage than the girl had, but after a moment's agonised hesitation she managed it. Ulysses behaved like the gentleman he was and, for the first time in Anna's acquaintance with her, Denise's sullen face broke into a warm, delighted grin. At this moment Hugo arrived, and thanked Anna so brusquely for her help that she thought Judith's claim against her could scarcely have seemed more ill-founded.

When they'd gone, Anna rang Fairhaven again to talk to Hubner. "Hugo and Denise have just left. Could I talk to you alone some time?"

He came an hour later, and she slowly described all that had been happening. Harriet's anonymous letter, the whispering campaign against herself, Michael's encounter with Mrs Hughes-Watson and finally, her conversation with Denise that morning.

"Does it seem far-fetched to think that all these things are related – orchestrated, even?" she finished up anxiously. "I can't help feeling that they are."

"How could they *not* be," he said with rare grimness. "There's an English saying – something about shutting the stable door after the horse has bolted! It's what I've almost allowed to happen, I'm afraid, but I think I can still do something about it before it's too late."

She didn't ask what it was, but had one more thing to say herself. "I'm now regarded as some sort of scarlet woman in the neighbourhood, thanks to Judith and her friends. But I realise that the fault has been partly mine. I should have taken more account of Hugh Town's different standards. Why should they accept London ways? This is their place, not mine. The harm is done now, and I shall probably go away when the Scillies book is finished, but I hope I shall be able to come back one day, and find *you* still here . . . still the dearest of my friends."

She saw the sternness in his face melt into such love and longing that she felt close to tears, but he answered steadily.

"Always your friend, however long it takes you to come back. But don't rush across the sea just yet, please. It may be that you don't need to go at all."

He smiled but didn't explain himself, and then went back to Fairhaven. It took an hour in his study, searching through current medical journals, but at last he found what he was looking for.

Fourteen

Judith hesitated at the sight of him standing in her doorway. He didn't seek her company as a rule, and their consulations about the running of the home usually took place on neutral ground. Always courteous, he'd still managed to give the impression that he didn't like her.

"Good morning, Judith. May I come in?" He decided to misread the cause of her hesitation. "You look doubtful. Perhaps I shouldn't call on you here. I – what is the expression in English? – endanger your reputation?"

"Nonsense," she said quickly. "I suppose you've come to talk about Denise; we're fortunate that she was found safe and sound."

"She also," he agreed pleasantly, following her into the small sitting-room that she looked upon as hers. "But in fact I came about this." He pulled a journal out of his pocket and pointed to an advertisement which had been outlined in red ink. It seemed that she was intended to read it and her eyes skimmed over the paragraph. It described a vacant post, supervising a large private clinic in Tangiers – the sort of establishment that catered exclusively for the rich and mighty. The job sounded exacting, but the fringe benefits appeared to be endless, and the salary offered was about four times the figure an English hospital superintendent could hope to earn.

"Very tempting," Judith commented with a smile, "but I'm not sure why you're showing it to me, except to make my mouth water!"

Hubner's face expressed nothing but detached interest. "You're wasted here. You should be running something like that, not our little affair. Worthwhile jobs aren't hard to find, but ones as generously rewarded as this certainly are."

"You don't have to tell me," she replied feelingly. "But as it happens, my next job is already lined up. In case you've forgotten, I'm about to marry Hugo!"

Still only friendly concern seemed to tinge Hubner's voice. "Hugo is very happy here, but you less so, I think. Perhaps you *should* look for another job."

She was puzzled by his insistence, but not yet alarmed. "If you're implying that I don't want to spend the rest of my life here, you're quite right. Hugo knows I want him to consider moving to somewhere a little more challenging; but I can't see him settling for Tangiers. This sort of medicine isn't his scene at all, I'd say."

"I agree with you," Peter Hubner said warmly. "What I had in mind was that you might want to go alone."

The tone of his voice still hadn't changed, but imperceptibly the atmosphere in the room had. She stared at him, refusing to feel frightened. "I don't understand you. We seem to be going round in circles."

"Then I shall come straight to the point. I think you should sacrifice your engagement and apply at once for this new job. It will be much sought after, but our references combined with your ability and outstanding looks ought to ensure that you get it."

"You're mad," she said flatly, "and a fine friend into the bargain. What would Hugo say, I wonder, if he could hear this conversation?"

"I'm not thinking about Hugo," his friend said untruthfully. "It's Hugh Town I have in mind, as a matter of fact. It seems to me that it would be a happier place without you."

"And if I say I don't care tuppence how anything seems to you?"

"Then I'm afraid our discussion becomes less pleasant. I should have to warn you of Robin Grayson's intention to sue you for libel, and of the fact that Michael Harding and I would both testify that you've been spreading false reports damaging to us as well as to Anna. Worst of all, professionally speaking, I should report that for purposes of your own you've deliberately manipulated an already unstable and unhappy child."

She stared at his implacable face, wondering how she could ever have seen him as a man too easy-going and pleasant to be reckoned with. It was an error of judgement that she wouldn't have made earlier in her career; she'd let herself grow careless. But an error was all it was – nothing to ruin her plans.

"You're bluffing," she said with confidence. "You've

got no shred of proof for any of this rubbish, and Hugo would never believe a word of it."

Hubner shook his head, almost sadly. "You repeated yourself, Judith – always a mistake, I believe. You shouldn't have played the same old trick of the anonymous letter on Harriet. That *was* how you got William to marry you, wasn't it? Hugo *will* believe me when he knows that."

The silence in the room bore down on them both, but most nerve-rackingly on Judith. She wasn't beaten yet, but she was beginning to feel afraid. "You know nothing about William," she tried to insist. "You *can't* do."

"He confided in Simon Redfern before he went to Africa. You know as well as I do that he was desperate to get away from you. Hugo could never have persuaded him not to go."

Her face was suddenly no longer beautiful; she looked older than her years, and the change tempered Hubner's distaste with pity. But what he'd begun had to be finished now. "I expect Denise wrote the letter to Harriet at your suggestion, but I doubt if you'd shelter behind her; in fact I'm sure you wouldn't. So take my advice, Judith, and leave Hugh Town; you can find an excuse for going, and Hugo needn't know about the lies and innuendos. You won't destroy *us* by staying, but I'm very much afraid that you'll destroy yourself."

"The psychiatrist's diagnosis! I think I can do without it," she said contemptuously. "It's only text-book stuff anyway. What do you know about the sort of life Denise Trotter and I know . . . ? About having to claw your way up from the bottom of the heap with no help from anyone else? If I decide to leave it will be because I can't wait to shake the dust of this damned sanctimonious place off my feet. You're welcome to it, and to Anna Carteret as well – always supposing that she gives up waiting for Hugo to notice her and settles for you instead as the best she can hope for."

The bitter jibe had no effect that she could see; the man in front of her merely gave a little bow as if she'd just paid him a compliment of some kind. "I suggest the *Scillonian* this afternoon then. Glowing professional references will be ready for you in an hour's time, and I shall compose them in the belief that you realise you can't afford to repeat any of your recent mistakes. Would you like *me* to explain to Hugo that the advancement of your career overrode your affection for him?"

She was tempted, he thought, to grab the nearest hard object and hurl it at him, but with an effort he had to admire she regained her self-control. "Explain *nothing*; I'll do it myself. Now, just get out."

Hubner bowed again and did as he was told. Relief at having won without more of a struggle to make her go was uppermost, but the taste of that interview was like gall in his mouth, and he thought it almost certain that whatever explanation she left behind would be aimed at wrecking his own friendship with Hugo. If so, it was a price he would have to pay.

Left alone, Judith struggled again not to let sheer rage overcome her; now wasn't the time to rail at fate or call down curses on the men who'd beaten her with the weapon they always relied on – hanging together in a way that women rarely seemed to manage. She'd been right to dread Simon Redfern's visit, but it was a bitter shock to discover that he'd known of something she herself had almost succeeded in forgetting. The letter to Harriet Grayson *had* been written by Denise, only too happy to have the idea put into her head of taking part in an exciting conspiracy. But a disturbed teenager wasn't to be depended upon; it wouldn't take much for her to transfer her doubtful affections to Anna Carteret, who would surely then learn the whole story. The letter had been a mistake, but it had worked so well with William that she'd been tempted into repeating it.

She didn't intend to make another mistake now and underestimate the Austrian. For all his seeming gentleness, there appeared to be a streak of steel in him that matched her own. If she refused to leave, he would talk to Hugo and, without thinking about it too closely, she realised that an interview with Hugo was something she would rather forego. The thought of failure was heart-breaking, and it meant yet another fresh start against younger competition. But she'd get the job somehow; she was a past mistress of making herself agreeable when it mattered, and Hubner would be careful to provide the sort of references that no appointing committee could afford to overlook. His own medical connections were impressive, and his social ones dazzling. Doktor Graf von Hubner's recommendation would carry the sort of weight that other candidates would find it hard to match. Judith looked again at the description of the job and came at last to the conclusion that, all things considered, she could do a lot worse than settle for Tangiers.

She hurried through the packing of her clothes and personal belongings, then sat down to write two important letters. The first, to Hugo, explained that she was being driven away by the malice of people who called themselves his friends. She thought with relish that it was an accusation he'd have to believe – he'd been embarrassed by their lack of enthusiasm about her. In their vendetta against her, she explained, they were even prepared to manufacture evidence which she felt too disheartened to stay and disprove. She ventured to repeat her suggestion that he should rid himself of certain people – especially of Peter Hubner, who seemed now to have successfully displaced Anna Carteret's London lover. Studying it carefully, she thought the letter was perfect in tone: brief, wistful and dignified.

The next one was even more crucial and took longer to write; she had to make several false starts before she was satisfied with it.

Dear Anna,

Forgive me for leaving without saying goodbye; one hates to be discourteous, but work is more important than anything else – not quite so true of your little bits of painting, perhaps, but I expect you're attached to them even so. I've had the offer of an assignment abroad so wonderfully exciting that nothing can be allowed to stand in its way. This will be a blow to poor, dear Hugo – he has such a physical thing about me; you had a chance to notice that once, and I'm bound to say he was rather a satisfying lover! But the truth is that I was beginning to find Hugh Town terribly cramping.

You seem able to put up with it yourself, so may I offer a parting word of advice? You're accustomed to living in a big city where no one cares what anyone else is doing; but take my word for it, that free and easy behaviour simply won't do here. However much you enjoy your reputation as a femme fatale, it really isn't wise to have a procession of admirers coming in and out of your cottage.

I only give you this hint because I know Hugo himself would do it if he felt brave enough. He has this rather absurd compulsion to take care of everyone in sight, so it wouldn't surprise me if he finished up by asking *you* to marry him. Fatal, my dear! A doctor's wife must be like the lady in the Bible – absolutely above reproach. Anyway, what woman would want to be 'saved' by marriage; it would be the kiss of death from the start.

Now, I really must fly. With every good wish,

Judith

She re-read the letter, then folded it with a sigh of satisfaction. It paid off every arrear of malice; even made up for her humiliation at Hubner's hands. When the taxi-driver arrived to take her to the quay, she gave him the envelope and asked him to deliver it personally to Anna's door. Then, with her testimonial and a generous cheque 'in lieu of notice', she left Fairhaven, permitting herself no backward glance; what would happen to it now she neither knew nor cared.

She was already on board the steamer by the time Anna, returning from an afternoon walk with Ulysses, took the letter out of her letter box. She opened it unthinkingly, read it, and fled to the bathroom to be immediately sick. When she emerged again Ulysses was waiting, ready to push his cold nose against her hand, and she touched it without knowing that she did so.

She forced herself to read the letter again, still for the moment scarcely taking in the astonishing fact that Judith had left the island. Every knife-prick found its mark and she felt sick again to know the full extent to which she had been hated. But worse, much worse, was the knowledge that Hugo had discussed her with this woman. She flayed herself by imagining the two of them together, wringing their hands over her stupidity as well as her laxness – the silly London creature who'd thought she could flaunt a small community's fixed ideas of what constituted acceptable behaviour. Tears of anguished rage trickled down her face as she marched about the room, with Ulysses trotting by her side to show that he was anxious to share her agitation.

"How dared he talk about me to that woman! How *could* he, Ulysses?" she demanded of her friend. But he could offer no excuse, and confined himself to licking her hand.

Anna smiled at him through her tears, aware that it was time to face the truth of what ailed her. She'd known it in her heart since the night of Rupert's visit when she'd been forced to measure him against Hugo. In a strange, unhappy way her reputation as a femme fatale had become a smokescreen since then. If she was known to be some sort of lurid nymphomaniac, she wouldn't have given herself away that day on Tresco; Hugo would have merely recognised her overriding urge to snare a male. He *had* recognised it, and almost responded to it – no doubt to later self-disgust.

She'd done her damnedest after that to stay clear of him, but Judith had known. Presumably another woman involved with the same man always *would* know and correctly read such signs. She brushed aside the letter's hint that Hugo might offer to make her respectable; one salvage marriage had ended in tragedy – it would have been enough even for a man so hell-bent on rescuing people.

Calm at last, she finally got round to considering the fact that Judith had gone. Peter Hubner had had something to do with it almost certainly, even at the cost of whatever grief it might cause his friend. Harriet at least would be overjoyed, and she herself could retire into solitude again. If she lived the life of a hermit from now on her bohemian reputation might subside enough for her neighbours to forget that she was there at all.

She steeled herself to go out as usual next morning, but felt convinced that her arrival in the shops interrupted at least two conversations. It required stubbornness to behave normally, not to fly home as if she had something to be ashamed of. But she got back to the cottage with nerve-ends jangling, wondering whether life there was ever going to be anything but this endurance test.

It was scarcely the best moment to find Hugo waiting on her doorstep, in full and brazen view of every passer-by. Her heart missed a beat at the sight of him, but she told herself that it was due to nothing more disturbing than blind rage. She must recover from loving him as best she could, but time was needed . . . Long months and years of *not* bumping into him every time she turned a corner or climbed into a boat or opened her front door.

"I didn't ask you to call – I'm not ill," she said flatly, trying to restrain Ulysses from lavishing an ill-timed welcome on his friend.

"I know . . . this is a purely social visit. I promised Emily I'd remind you about her birthday party on Saturday."

"I hadn't forgotten, and in any case Harriet telephoned this morning. There was no need for you to come." There was no welcome for him either, her tone indicated, and his strong suspicion was that as soon as she opened the door she would close it behind her, leaving him outside.

"It's a long walk down from the top of the hill," he suggested gravely. "Shouldn't I be allowed to come in and recover before toiling up again?"

Her unresponsive face confirmed that she wasn't amused, and he couldn't blame her – their acquaintance had been chequered from the start, perhaps nearly ruined by the interference of other people. But he knew what she *didn't* know; he was a free, unencumbered man again, and instinct and need alike had driven him at once to seek her out.

"I'm sorry I didn't thank you properly at the time for taking care of Denise for us," he said next. "Peter Hubner has been with her quite a lot since then. He thinks he's got a good chance now of straightening her out. She's very taken with you by the way."

Anna merely answered with a token bow, determined not to get into any conversation that would have to include the name of Judith Jackson. Hugo looked at her unyielding expression and pierced her with his next rueful question.

"Are you really in such a hurry to get rid of me as I seem to imagine?"

She heard such sadness in his voice that she almost capitulated; but the terms of Judith's letter were etched in acid on her memory and kept her resolute.

"I'm very busy," she pointed out, calm and cool until his raised eyebrow suddenly catapulted her into anger. "Even we brothel ladies have our off days, so excuse me if I don't ask you in. I expect that *is* what you came to find out – whether or not I'm entertaining an admirer on the premises?"

There was nothing in his face now except an anger to match her own. "Do you mind telling me what all this is about, preferably a little less publicly than on your doorstep?"

"Why not just accept the fact that I've got work to do? You might also give a thought to your own reputation – I know you're concerned about mine; but doctors have to be especially careful, so I'm told."

"Damn my reputation, Anna," he said furiously.

"And as I understand it, you're never too busy to see other people."

"Ah. I thought we'd come to that. With Judith gone, who else will you find, I wonder, to lament my immoral ways with?" The expression on his face almost halted her, but she rushed desperately on. "You did discuss me with her – *didn't* you?"

Unable to lie, even though every instinct warned him that he would always regret not doing so, he agreed stiffly that her name had cropped up between them. He even made matters worse by insisting that Judith's concern had been genuine when she warned him that comings and goings at the cottage were offending people.

"You need worry no longer," Anna said coldly. "I'm a reformed character from now on. At home to no one – beginning with you."

She dragged Ulysses inside and closed the door, leaving Hugo to climb the hill again, seeing nothing as he went but her eyes brilliant with unshed tears.

In the heat of the moment he'd scarcely registered what she'd said; now he realised that Judith must have written to her as well as to himself. He could make a guess at the letter's terms, and see the pit he had just dug for himself. What, if anything, could be done about it he didn't know, but first he must wring the truth of Judith's departure out of Peter Hubner.

In the following days, morbidly convinced that everyone was watching her, Anna buried herself in work and hid alike from friend and foe. Nature helped by seeming to share her mood of tormented sadness, and in the autumn gales that began to sweep over the islands it was hard to remember the sun-shot beauty of midsummer. At least, though, she could now provide what the publishers had asked for – a nearly year-round picture of this ocean-pounded, wind-torn habitat.

With the idea of completeness in mind, she embarked on a series of uncomfortable trips and brought back marvellous images to try and realise in paint. She braved a visit to the seaward side of Bryher to see what Hell Bay looked like when a westerly gale was blowing, and came back not only drenched to the skin but convinced that the place had been correctly named. She went northwards to Round Island on another rough day, and saw the terrifying race of water through the narrow channel between Round Island and St Helen's – a nightmare vision that the lighthouse crew must have to stare at through all the hours of daylight.

Encouraged by the fact that she had managed this horrendous journey without being seasick, she persuaded the skipper of the next boat going out to the Bishop lighthouse to let her go too, and she was so entranced by the sight of it ringed by fountains of glistening spray that she forgot to be frightened of the seas around her.

Nature's storms were fearsome, but they weren't individually hostile or personal in their intention to cause damage; it was the unkindness of other human beings that Anna now shrank from. She even got to the point of neglecting her friends until Harriet pursued her home one morning and insisted on being allowed inside the cottage.

"You haven't been near us for days," Harriet said reproachfully. "As far as I know, we're not infectious, and the girls are getting very hurt."

Anna looked at her friend's transparent face and had the grace to feel ashamed of herself. "Sorry, Harriet . . . I've been silly. But having got the idea that *I* was infectious, or *persona non grata* at least, I found it easier to stay away from people than pretend I didn't notice them backing away from me."

"What a bitch Judith was," Harriet said simply. "Thank God she's gone away."

"Well, yes . . . but I don't see how her going will improve anyone's feelings towards me."

Harriet stared at her blankly. "But she has everything to do with it . . . Didn't Peter tell you?"

"I've been avoiding him too," Anna confessed. "I stopped going to Fairhaven – said I couldn't spare the time."

"Well, we'll talk about it now, and then consider the whole sordid subject closed. Judith wanted to get rid of you because Hugo enjoyed your company and appreciated your work. She was at the bottom of all the trouble, including the letter to me about Robin and you which she inspired poor little Denise to write. A few of her cronies were ready to persuade themselves that what she said about you was true, but without her, the gossip will die a natural death and we can all be happy again."

Anna hovered on the edge of denying it – happiness was a will-o'-the-wisp, all too easily deflected or destroyed. Not even to Harriet could she admit that her last error looked like being worse and more painful than her first. It was lunacy in spades to have ended up loving a large, puritan-minded Highlander who saw her as a fallen woman to be saved. She'd frequently lashed herself with the thought that if he'd come before Judith's letter arrived she might have blithely hauled him inside, confirming that she was ripe and ready for the first man who called.

The bleakness in her face made Harriet suddenly enfold her in a warm hug. "Don't look like that, Anna. I know that damned woman damaged us, one way and another, but it's nothing we can't get over, you'll see."

Anna smiled and agreed. It was something, at least, to know that distrust and disapproval had been deliberately manufactured. She wasn't as optimistic as her friend that ill-will would blow away like a morning's sea mist, but after Harriet's visit she felt more determined about behaving normally. With courage buckled on like armour, she went shopping at busy times when she was likely to meet people she knew, and it was a relief – even something of an anticlimax – to find that no one took any special notice of her. Perhaps she'd never been quite the figure of public notoriety that a fevered imagination had led her to believe.

She came out of the supermarket one morning to untie Ulysses from the railing and found herself face to face with a woman who had frequently avoided her in the past. This time Mrs Hughes-Watson made no attempt to walk away; she was clinging to Ulysses' collar with one hand, and holding his broken leash with the other.

"He'd got loose. I was afraid he'd run into the road and be hurt," she explained jerkily, not looking at Anna.

It wasn't the moment to insist that Ulysses was much too clever to do anything so foolish. "I'm very grateful," Anna said instead, meaning it. "I can't imagine what I'd do without him."

The woman's wandering gaze suddenly came to rest on Anna's face. "I know . . . I had a retriever once . . . One gets stupidly attached to them."

She nodded and walked away, leaving Anna with the feeling that the brief encounter hadn't gone unnoticed. It was irritating in a way, that rather public rehabilitation by a woman she would probably never like; but at least it seemed to signal the beginning of a return to normality. She could go on living in Hugh Town after all – even if the thought of sharing it, however remotely, with Hugo was only just bearable. He would probably leave before too long in any case. There was no permanent job for him in St Mary's.

Immediately, though, she could and must now change her mind about attending the opening of the children's painting exhibition which she'd been intending to avoid. When she rang Peter Hubner to tell him so, she imagined she could see his wry smile.

"I know you've been trying to make yourself invisible lately, but you weren't going to be allowed to stay away. I had strict instructions from the children – you were to be there, dragged if necessary, for a 'very perticler' reason!"

*   *   *

The exhibition, over which she and Robin had laboured with such care, was held in the Town Hall in the main square for the whole of one weekend. It was officially opened by the Mayor. Everybody came and nothing remained unsold at the end of it, to the children's astonished delight.

Their 'perticler' need to have Anna present was made clear at the end of the opening ceremony. She was given an enormous bouquet and a thank-you card that was the combined effort of all her pupils. She accepted both gifts rather tearfully, amid much applause, and couldn't help shooting a rueful smile at Peter Hubner for the unpredictable ups and downs of public popularity. His answering grin, confirming that he knew what she was thinking, was intercepted by at least one other member of the audience. Their shared glance had been full of understanding and affection, and there wasn't one good reason why it shouldn't be, Hugo admitted painfully to himself. He'd known for long enough what his friend felt about Anna Carteret, and it now looked as if Judith had been right: Rupert Neville's image had finally been blotted out by a quiet, charming Austrian who deserved all the joy Anna would give him.

Hugo promised himself that he would smile and wish them well when the time came, but he made an excuse to leave now as soon as the Mayor's speech was over. He'd agreed to buy whatever the children selected for him, and afterwards he found himself the owner of a spirited rendering of an animal so strange-looking that only the title gave him a clue.

Not sure of the correct spelling of the creature's name, the artists had sensibly settled for something they could manage – 'Anna's dog'. It would go with him from now on wherever he went, and he'd never be able to explain what it meant to him.

Fifteen

With her visits to Fairhaven and the Graysons resumed, Anna had no reason to feel lonely. She told herself repeatedly in fact that she had every reason to be content all round. The Scillies book was nearly ready, *would* be ready in time; and Elizabeth Harding had promised to deliver it in the course of the pre-Christmas trip she always made to London. After that there were more commissions waiting – among them illustrations for a series of children's books so enchantingly written that working on them would seem nothing but pure pleasure.

With her blessings counted yet again, to overcome the depression that nevertheless kept waiting to creep up on her, she set off as usual for Fairhaven one afternoon and met Morag Robertson on the way. Morag greeted her and seemed for once not determined to hurry off to prepare the doctor's next meal – what was on the rota for his Friday supper, Anna wondered but didn't like to ask. The question was answered for her when Morag pointed to the grey water that heaved in Porthcressa's usually peaceful bay.

"It'll be a rough crossing, I'm thinking, but Dr Hugo won't mind that; he's a braw sailor."

In her estimate he'd be braw at anything, Anna realised; braving Hell or storming Heaven would be child's play for Hugo McKay in the opinion of this devoted woman.

"A day-trip to Penzance for the doctor, Morag?" she asked lightly.

"Och no, lassie. He's away to London. Been fretting, he has, to get back to work. I dinna ken when we'll see him here again."

Nothing had changed; the afternoon *hadn't* got dark and miserably cold just because an ill-tempered Highlander had left the island without even bothering to say goodbye. She parted company with Morag, sounding wonderfully cheerful, she thought. But walking on alone again, it would have been a relief to sit by the roadside and weep her tears away.

At Fairhaven, she took her usual warm interest in the work the children had prepared, shared tea with them and the pleasant woman who had taken Judith's place, and felt aggrieved when Peter Hubner asked her afterwards what was troubling her.

"Nothing. Nothing at all," she said sharply. "I can't smile *all* the time – it's tiring, and rather pointless, too." The sound of her voice, petulant and unfamiliar, seemed to echo round the room, shaming her into an apology. "Sorry . . . I think I must be sickening for a cold; it always makes me irritable."

He shook his head, and she realised that her second lie had achieved as little as the first – he hadn't believed either of them.

"I can't help knowing when you're unhappy," he

said simply. "If I knew *why*, I might be able to do something about it . . . at least, I hope so."

She was able to smile now, for the sheer unselfish goodness of the man. "Indeed you might, if I properly knew why myself." That was yet another untruth – she was becoming a habitual liar, it seemed. But his eyes were on her face and she feared that a leap of intuition would allow him to land on the truth. Well, part of it she could safely offer him – and, at last, admit to herself.

"I arrived at St Mary's miserable and unwell. I got better, and loved being here so much that I felt heart-sick when it looked as if I wasn't welcome to stay. Now that it seems I *am*, I'm not sure I want to – human nature being nothing if not perverse! This is a *lovely* little world, Heaven knows, and I shall miss a hundred things about it if I go away; but I think I *shall* leave soon, before I lose my nerve for travelling in the fast lane!"

She felt pleased with that – it sounded honest but not too rueful, feisty enough, in today's silly feminist phrase, to convince him that he needn't worry about her. His face didn't warn her of what he was going to say next.

"Fast lane or slow, I doubt if that counts for much," he said quietly. "It's travelling alone or not that decides our happiness. Harriet could become a fashionable, famous potter outside the islands, but her true happiness is being here with Robin and the children. It's the people we set our hearts on that matter, nothing else."

Anna was silent for a moment before she answered him with a question. "What about *your* loneliness?"

"Visible sometimes, I expect," he admitted with a faint smile. He held out his hands suddenly and she was obliged to put her own cold ones into his warm grasp. They felt better like that – someone else's touch, love, offered strength, shared laughter – these were the important things, not the lane she travelled in. He sensed her small response and seized a chance that might not come again.

"My darling, I said it once before, though not very well, because the words I need are in my own language; but let me try again, please, because I shan't say this to any other woman. There's no grief or pain or loneliness I couldn't gladly bear with you, and I would try until my life's end to make *you* happy."

Anna smiled at him unsteadily. "That *might* sound more beautiful in German, but I doubt it."

"It requires *you* to say something," he pointed out gently.

She nodded, looking at a vision of the future that seemed vague in every way except in its promise of almost certain solitariness; there wasn't any doubt about that. Hugo had gone, uncaringly as far as she was concerned. The needy multitudes of Africa would soon swallow him up if he could talk some lunatic panel of doctors into allowing him to go back. If not, he'd fashion a life somewhere else that still didn't include her. The vision was so bleak that she wrenched her inward eye away from it and looked at the man in front of her instead. He was right about Harriet – loving and being loved kept *her* happy here. He was right about most things; if she said she wasn't in love with him his smile would promise that it didn't matter, and he'd probably be right about that, too.

"I'm going to London to spend Christmas with Aunt Agatha," she said at last. "I think I'll know then what I should do. If I do come back here it will be to share your loneliness. For the moment, will that do?"

A smile lit his face at the grave question. "*Liebchen*, it will do very well."

The conversation ended there, and they didn't refer to it again as the days – depending on who was counting – limped or galloped towards Christmas. The Grayson children protested every time Anna saw them that she was required to worship at the manger with *them*, not go rushing back to London. But she was anxious to get away now – clinging to the idea that in her aunt's caustic, unsentimental company she would finally be able to decide what to do.

But the weather was becoming increasingly wild, and even if the *Scillonian* managed to keep sailing, she visualised a nightmare journey, with Ulysses – a fair-weather sailor at the best of times – howling his displeasure all the way to Penzance.

Then, the quiet routine of one mid-December afternoon was interrupted by a sound she'd heard often enough before when the lifeboat crew practiced – the urgent whine of the station siren; but this time the streams of people hurrying past the cottage seemed to signal that a rehearsal was *not* getting under way. She threw on a coat and hurried out to join the rest of the town watching the boat being launched. The team of local men went calmly but swiftly about a

195

ritual which practice had long since made perfect. The boat's skipper, Anna's favourite among the boatmen she'd got to know all summer, was immediately recognisable by his flaming red beard. Another figure, larger than most, was similarly kitted out in the anonymous yellow oilskins but, with a sudden stoppage of her heartbeat, she had no difficulty in identifying *him* either.

Why or when Hugo had come back she didn't know, but he was indisputably there, in time to share in whatever triumph or disaster was about to happen – imposters both of *them*, according to Rudyard Kipling, she found herself remembering numbly. She'd always been inclined to think that poets saw and spoke the truth; but Kipling hadn't known about Hell Bay's rocks and tumultuous seas where the knowledgeable among the crowd said that a stricken coaster was in trouble.

Like the rest of the watchers on the shore, she lifted her hand in a little salute as, fully manned now, the boat raced down the long ramp and dived into the sea. She supposed that, like her, the others offered up a prayer to bring it safely home again. The lifeboat was out of sight within a minute or two, lost in the blur of wind and rain. She turned blindly away and cannoned into someone else. It was Morag, watching the doctor out of sight. She blinked at Anna and hastily mopped at the tears and rain drops on her face.

"I've seen them go times without number, lassie, but I never get used to it."

"What about coming home with me for a cup of

tea?" Anna suggested. "I dare say there'll be a long wait ahead of us."

Morag nodded and summoned up a smile. "Aye, long enough. A cup of tea meanwhile would be verra welcome."

They fought their way back to the cottage against the wind and, with both of them leaning on the front door, got it shut in the teeth of the gale blowing straight in from the sea. Anna lit the fire, made tea and, anxious to divert Morag's mind from what was going on at Hell Bay, showed her the material that had gone towards making the final draft of the Scillies book.

"I had nothing to do with writing the words," she explained. "It was Michael Harding who did that for me."

Morag clucked, marvelled, and identified people and places with great relish. "It'll be a mairsterpiece," she decided finally with a simple conviction that defied for it the possibility of any other fate.

"Not quite that, I'm afraid, but at least I hope it will be worth the trouble it seems to have caused," Anna pointed out. The moment to raise an awkward subject had arisen naturally, and she was determined not to let it slip. "It was Dr Hubner's idea in the first place, and he and Mr Harding have often been here to talk about it with me. I'm afraid their visits were misunderstood by some of my neighbours; I was stupid not to realise that they would be."

Morag's reply was, first, a contemptuous snort. "No misunderstanding, lassie," she said next. "It was just wicked spite at work. But there. Yon besom's gone now; you'll not need to worry any more."

"I didn't realise Hugo was back," Anna said next, unable at last not to mention him. "You didn't expect him so soon, I imagine."

"No. I was happy to see him, of course, but I wish he'd stayed away longer now – though I should be ashamed of saying that when there may be puir, damaged men out there needing him."

She refused Anna's suggestion that she should stay, insisting that her place was beside the doctor's telephone; there was no telling who might be asking for him. Anna watched her go – anxious but indomitable – then threw herself into a mad house-cleaning session that she could remember nothing about afterwards.

The early winter darkness fell but it seemed unbearable to stay in doors. She put on coat and scarf again and fought her way back to the knot of people still clustered round the lifeboat station. There was no hard fact available, just conjecture, sad reminiscences of similar waits in the past and one rumour after another being murmured round the crowd: the coaster had already sunk; had broken in two; was still afloat. The possibilities went back and forth, a feverish counterpoint to the continual racket of the wind and the thump of the sea against the enclosing arm of the bay. The time passed slowly, and it seemed to Anna as if the whole of her life had been spent standing there. Nothing now might *ever* change; perhaps she must spend the rest of her life waiting for a man who didn't arrive. The possibility led her to the certainty of something else: there was no need to go to London after all to make up her mind, only the need to leave and stay away. Like Peter Hubner's, her heart couldn't change; but to remain here and not marry him would be too cruel. To London she would have to go.

Then a rumour almost more dreadful than the rest penetrated the thoughts she'd been wrapped in. The coaster *was* still afloat, but only just. Most of the crew had been lifted off, and the lifeboat was on its way back to St Mary's; but there were two seamen too injured to be moved in present conditions. What remained of the ship was caught in a cleft of the rock it had foundered on, and it had been decided to leave them where they were for the time being. The coaster's skipper was staying with them . . . and so, of course, was the doctor.

The man standing beside Anna turned to her and found something to say. "I thought Hugo'd stay . . . he *would*, wouldn't he?"

She agreed politely, weeping her heart's tears in silence. Yes, he'd stay. Oh God, of course he would.

The boat came back half an hour later, with a dozen soaked and shocked survivors on board, in addition to its own exhausted crew. She searched fruitlessly among the anonymous yellow-suited figures, though she knew the man she looked for wouldn't be there. The rumour was true – Hugo was still out in that raging mass of water, on the wreck of what had probably been an ill-found sieve of a ship to begin with. She waited only to hear that the lifeboat would go out again at first light, and then battled her way up the hill to the doctor's house; Morag had the door open before she was halfway up the path.

"They're back with most of the survivors," Anna said, marvelling at the calmness of her voice. "Hugo's still on the coaster, though, with two badly injured men; the boat will try to bring them off tomorrow."

She might, she thought, have been describing a routine trip to pick up letters, or a light-hearted pleasure outing. Morag looked in silence at the stricken face in front of her; then she managed a confident smile.

"We'll see him then, lassie, never fear. Just think how thankful those poor men must be to have him with them." She looked out at the cloud-tossed sky, and confidence wavered for a moment. "The good Lord's got to do something about this tairrible wind, though."

Her faith in Hugo was absolute, Anna realised, and in the Almighty almost as unshakeable; but she saw no harm in bringing to His attention a matter he mustn't be allowed to overlook.

With a shy kiss dropped on Morag's cheek, she struggled back to her own home, to spend the rest of the night crouched by the fire, making sketch after sketch of Hugo's face. If she had seen him for the last time, it would be unbearable in future years not to be able to remember exactly how a lock of dark hair always fell over his forehead, or the way the forbidding planes of his face changed when he began to smile.

She fell into an exhausted doze towards dawn, and woke an hour later, stiff and cold, to a more peaceful world. The Lord in His infinite mercy had heard Morag's reminder; but in the grey light outside her window the seas beyond the harbour pool looked just as mountainous, and she was familiar enough now with the island waters to know that days of calm weather would be needed to quieten them. She bathed and dressed, fed Ulysses and made coffee for herself; then once more headed in the direction of the lifeboat station.

The boat had already left, and now she found Harriet in the clump of waiting people.

"Robin's in the relief crew," Harriet explained simply.

They linked arms for warmth and comfort, and stood staring out across the channel towards Bryher.

"The coaster's still above water," Harriet pointed out with determined cheerfulness.

"And the wind's less," Anna added as her own mite of encouragement. They tried to smile at each other, and said no more.

The men who had been out the previous day were already drifting back, unable to stay away until the boat was safely home again. They explained what they'd seen of the wreck; the rock on which the ship had been trapped held the stern half afloat, and it was in this precarious haven that they'd left Hugo and his patients. The time crawled past, but at last a shout went up.

"She's coming!"

Anna stared, swore soundlessly because she *couldn't* see for the tears that blinded her eyes . . . but yes, dear God, the boat *was* coming. She and Harriet moved mindlessly with the crowd as it appeared out of the spray fifty yards away from them. Then it was being winched up the ramp, stretchers lifted out and carried to the waiting ambulance. Anna saw Robin's fair head as he pushed off his sou-wester the better to kiss his wife; then a moment later she could see nothing else in the whole world because Hugo was standing in front of her. His face was bone-white with exhaustion and shadowed with the beginnings of a dark beard, but never, she thought, could Apollo have looked more beautiful.

"I'm glad you're back, Hugo," she said in a prim voice that barely shook at all.

His eyes seemed to have sunk back in their sockets, and she looked in vain for the smile that always began there. In the long anguish of the night she'd forgotten their last confrontation on the cottage doorstep. He was almost dead on his feet – she told herself she must remember that – but could he not have smiled and said hello? In the crowd of people that surrounded her she saw Harriet still arm-linked with Robin, and knew the full heart-breaking truth of what Hubner had said about loneliness. Without knowing that she did so, she lifted her hand in a little gesture of farewell that Hugo still didn't respond to. Then she walked away, unable to stay and look at him any longer.

A week later, with the sea no worse than usual for December, she boarded the *Scillonian* with Ulysses, and sat on deck watching the islands recede. She stared dry-eyed – because it was necessary to watch until the moment when they were no longer distinguishable from the greyness of water and sky.

London, when she reached it, seemed louder, more frantic than she could bear; the amplified roar of

'Jingle Bells' above the other racket of Paddington Station had nothing at all to do with the spirit of Christmas; she'd left that behind with the crib that Emily and Liza had made, inexpertly but with so much love.

Agatha Prescott welcomed her almost warmly and, after a glance at her white face, managed not to say that the other residents of the block of mansion-flats might soon be searching the small print of their letting agreements in the hope of finding that animals were not allowed. But as if understanding the limitations of the people who shared the lift with him, Ulysses behaved with such decorum that they began to pat his head; only later, out on Hampstead Heath did he leap and bark and become the dog he was. Anna knew how he felt; she felt just as cribbed, cabined and confined herself.

She was grateful for her aunt's company, but as soon as the long Christmas break was over she would find herself a flat – somewhere on the outskirts of the metropolis, where she could afford the rent, and Ulysses wouldn't have to pretend to be scarcely visible at all.

Sixteen

The new year was a day old when Peter Hubner received the letter Anna had delayed writing in London. He thought he could guess what it would say. If she'd been going to spend the rest of her life with him on St Mary's, she'd have come in person to tell him so. He'd often visualised that moment – opening the door one day to find her there, smiling at him.

The letter was read and put away by the time Hugo walked in. He looked happy to be leaving again, but Hubner understood why. Uncertainty had been hard to live with, but now at least his future was fixed. It wasn't to be the return to Zambia he'd hoped for, but he'd throw himself into the running of a huge mainland hospital instead.

"We shall miss you," Peter Hubner said truthfully. "Small communities need a few people like you, larger than life and more awkward!" He smiled at the idea and his friend grinned back.

"Truro's not a million miles away," Hugo answered cheerfully. "I'll be back for the Easter break, God willing. No, I *must* get back – we shall have a lot to do here, you and I."

It was true, of course. Their latest project was the

building of another house in the grounds of Fairhaven, where the children could be moved as they grew old enough to live partially unsupervised. It was Hubner's idea, cherished for years, that his young patients should gradually learn to take responsibility for themselves, instead of becoming dependent on institutional care. The idea had been his, but it had needed Hugo's generosity and support to make it feasible. Watching the house take shape would be a daily solace – something positive to anchor sore heart and mind to.

"Anna isn't coming back," he said suddenly. He'd meant not to mention her, felt convinced that he wouldn't; but the words were out before he could stifle them, and he had to go on. "I thought there was a chance – that she'd hate London enough; but she sounds happy there."

He fiddled with the papers on his desk – always a neat, methodical man, but not one who normally rearranged things with this degree of mathematical precision. Hugo watched him, thinking that it would be a relief to be able to hate Anna Carteret.

"I'm sorry," he murmured. "It's a thousand pities that Agatha Prescott ever sent her here. She's a lorelei woman, enticing but heartless."

"*Not* perched on a rock in the Rhine," Hubner insisted with a wry smile, "and not heartless, either, but 'enticing' I'll grant you!" He stared at his friend's face, aware of never having been able to gauge Hugo's true opinion of the woman they were talking about, although he'd made a guess at it often enough. It almost certainly wasn't the one he'd just been offered.

Hugo didn't answer for a moment. Memory had pitchforked him back to the last time he'd seen her – standing on the quay after the lifeboat had come back. The picture of her in his mind's eye was still much too clear for comfort: tired and fine-drawn, she hadn't looked beautiful, but she was there, and he'd survived moments during the night when the chance of seeing her again had seemed very remote. The longing to wrap his arms round her, in front of half Hugh Town, had been almost more than he could manage; but she wasn't his – Hubner had been the man reeled in on her line. He'd had to let her walk away, unable even to speak to her. Harriet had referred only once since then to the incident, in terms that said she hadn't approved of his behaviour. But not even to her had he been able to explain.

He put the memory away, and offered the most convincing smile he could manage. "Time I was off, I think. Keep the pressure on the builders – we want the house ready this summer, not next."

"I shall be pleasant but firm." Hubner agreed. "*Auf wiedersehen*, Hugo."

Left alone, he almost took Anna's letter out again, then closed the drawer he'd half-opened and picked up a sheaf of papers instead. This was what he was here for, and there were case-notes to study of a boy who was being sent to Fairhaven in a day or two. It was the usual heart-breaking story of violence and neglect – a repetition of the cruelty that human beings too often offered each other. Fairhaven gave children like this one the first chance they'd ever had to break out of the vicious circle of their lives, and if his satisfaction in future was only to come from seeing *them* improve, it would have to be enough.

He gathered up the notes and went in search of the new matron. She hadn't said very much so far, but already the new atmosphere in the house pleased him. It meant that its inmates were accepting her. Optimism faltered for a moment when he passed the room where Anna had given her painting lessons, but he walked steadily on, ready to stop and talk to any of the children he met.

It was a miserable spring in London, either cold enough to be confused with winter or blustery and wet. Easter was late, and Anna was tempted to do what thousands of her compatriots were planning – find an aeroplane that would take her to southern warmth and sunlight. But the problem was Ulysses: she could find kennels that might be ready to accept a large, determined and apparently ill-trained animal, or she could implore him and Aunt Agatha to put up with one another while she went away; but neither solution appealed to her very much.

Easter was less than a week away and still she dithered. The lassitude that gripped her was to blame, she explained to her companionable hound; decisions, dates and details needed energy, and she had none to spare. But her aunt was forthright on the subject as usual.

"You work too hard, and you spend too much time cooped up here alone – it's the curse of people who are self-employed."

She had accepted Anna's airy statement that, though

lovely, the Fortunate Isles were a little too small and inward-looking for permanent habitation, and had never pointed out until now that her niece's London life scarcely seemed to enjoy any wider horizons. But whatever the problem that had sent her back to London, it must have cured itself by now, Agatha thought; she was a confirmed believer in doing nothing about her own aches and pains and uncertainties, and they always responded very well to this masterly inactivity. She stared now at Anna's white face and suddenly found herself repeating more or less the advice she'd given her once before. "The rhododendrons will be out on Tresco. Why not go and enjoy them, and make sure your cottage hasn't been blown into the sea?"

Anna inspected the idea. Why not go? Harriet's infrequent, scrawled letters confirmed that Hugo was no longer there, and Peter Hubner had written so calmly and kindly that, even if she bumped into him in the course of a brief visit, no harm would be done.

"Ulysses hates London parks," she admitted with a smile. "He makes little whinnying noises when he's asleep and I know he's back on Garrison again, chasing rabbits!" She looked at her aunt's dear, horse-like face. "You come too; we'd like you to."

"Bridge competition that I've a good chance of winning," Agatha said briskly. "Otherwise I would."

Three days later, ahead of the Easter exodus from London, Anna set off westward, with Ulysses howling mournfully in the guard's van. They arrived late in

Penzance, and spent the night there. In the morning the *Scillonian* was waiting in the harbour; by lunchtime a boisterous crossing had been survived by both of them and they were back in Hugh Town.

She walked along the main street, happy to discover that progress hadn't overtaken it since she was last there – pubs, shops and cottages, though being given a fresh coat of paint to welcome the new season, were just as she remembered them. The boards were out in the square, advertising the day's sailings, the seagulls were screaming a welcome from every rooftop perch and, at the end of small alley-ways leading to the harbour, lay the remembered hyacinth-coloured water – indigo mixed with cobalt mixed with violet that her paint-box had never quite managed to reproduce.

She was glad to be there. Glad to be home, her heart wanted to say. What she'd lost didn't make it any *less* but much more the place she would need to come back to from time to time. It was something that hadn't been understood when she went away, but the clear island light was all around her now, and at last she wasn't seeing life in a glass darkly any more.

Back at the cottage, with some shopping done on the way, she telephoned Harriet Grayson, who predictably announced at once that since all her friends would be invited to the pottery that evening *she* would be expected to be there. Anna agreed, but asked that she should be allowed to ring Fairhaven first herself.

Unable when it came to the point to announce her return in any way that seemed tactful, she blurted out – sounding like an embarrassed schoolgirl, she thought – the fact that she was briefly staying at the cottage. There was a moment's silence at the other end before Peter Hubner answered her in a voice that expressed only quiet pleasure. She had nothing to fear, it said. No repetition of the proposal she'd refused, no sense of guilt that need keep her away from them in future.

"Harriet's going to get on to you in a moment," she confessed hurriedly, thinking to give him notice of an invitation he might otherwise refuse, but this time he didn't even hesitate.

"Good, Anna; then there's a happy evening to look forward to. I shall bore you a little with news of Fairhaven, but not too much, I hope! What are you going to do this afternoon – let your misbegotten hound tow you round St Mary's? If so, you could call in here for tea."

She thanked him but heard herself make a choice that she hadn't even known was in her mind. It was to Tresco that she was going first; Ulysses would have to wait for his favourite walk on the home island.

Sitting beside the skipper of a nearly empty launch half an hour later, she occupied the brief trip by chatting to him about the past winter. He wasn't sorry it was over. Some people might pretend they disliked the visitors who returned with the swallows in the spring; but the truth was that, come Easter, they were a mite tired of talking to each other, and glad to see some fresh faces.

She left behind on the quay the handful of people she'd come over with and climbed the coastal path, with Ulysses making excited dashes into the bracken and honeysuckle. She could see his tail waving happily above the greenery, and every so often he'd come back to make sure he hadn't lost her, but he had affairs of his own to see to as well.

She stopped above the ruin of a Cromwellian castle, where the channel ran like a ribbon of blue silk between Tresco and its neighbouring island. It was a favourite vantage-point, but spoiled for her now by the fact that someone else had found it first and sat watching Bryher across the blue water, just as she'd meant to do. The man had dark, untidy hair, wore a rough sweater, looked as if he might be tall when he stood up – nothing very unusual in that; he could have been any one of the visitors that the boatmen had brought across that day. But he *wasn't* any visitor. He was, dear God, the only man she wasn't ready to see.

She stopped in her tracks, trying to force heart and lungs to behave normally. If she turned back Ulysses would eventually notice and come to find her. But he found the man first and went prancing up to him, tail wagging like a flag of victory, barks of delight insisting that he'd found a friend.

Hugo took time to greet him, knowing that the dog's owner couldn't now run away; then at last he turned to look at her, standing a dozen paces away, white-faced and silent, already made a little unfamiliar by having been reclaimed by her London life.

"Small world," he managed to say, chattily, he thought, as he might have greeted any acquaintance run into in some obscure corner of the globe.

"Very," she agreed. It wasn't a scintillating reply,

211

but the best she could do when her legs were trembling and her heart seemed to be leaping into her mouth. The conversation, if such it could be called, had come to a grinding halt, and she realised that some huge effort was now called for. "I thought you'd gone away . . . *left* the islands," she tried to make it clear.

"So did you," he pointed out. Then, when she wasn't ready for it, his sword lunged. "If Ulysses hadn't spotted me you'd have turned tail and run, but I was waiting for you to walk this way. Peter Hubner told me you were coming to Tresco, you see."

She wanted not to look at him, wanted to stare at the gorse blooming at her feet, at the blue sea and sky around them, but his face, not seen for weary months, kept getting in the way. It was what she'd spent the night of the shipwreck trying to draw, to remember him by – as if she could ever forget. It was her turn again to say something, but the words were lost in the tears that clogged her throat, and Hugo spoke again instead, almost roughly as if she were still at fault, still making him angry.

"I thought you'd forgotten Neville enough to accept what Peter Hubner offered you . . . He deserves to be happy, if ever a man did."

"I know. I *know* that." Had she shouted the words? "I do know that," she insisted more quietly. It seemed pointless to add that the memory of Rupert had almost faded from her mind. No, not pointless, dangerous; and she couldn't safely allow him to go on talking about herself. She plunged wildly instead into his own affairs. "You didn't get back to Africa then. I'm sorry – it's what you wanted."

"I make do with what I've got instead. It's no hardship to work in Truro, and have the rest of Cornwall on my doorstep. I expect *you're* enjoying London just as much."

They sounded, she thought, like characters in a Noel Coward play – 'and how *was* the Taj Mahal? Not like a biscuit-barrel, I hope.' She couldn't bear it any longer, and to get through the evening ahead would have to pray that Harriet didn't know he was back.

She signalled to her dog and he came at once as if sensing her desperate need. Then, with a shaking hand on his collar, she was able to smile at Hugo. "Ulysses isn't all that keen on the Great Wen, I'm afraid, but *I'm* glad to be back in the swim. *Au revoir*, Hugo; it's nice to have bumped into you again."

She lifted her free hand in a little wave and turned to leave, but his next question came floating on the air behind her, pinning her where she stood.

"Why did you choose Tresco this afternoon?"

Why indeed? The question had been haunting the margin of her mind, and she'd refused to acknowledge it. But the floodgates of memory were being swept aside now, like matchsticks in a stream; she was left with only the cold, dry ground of the truth to stand upon.

"I didn't choose . . . I just came. It's what animals do – return to a place where they've felt safe and happy."

Hugo came towards her, but stopped at arm's length, and his expressionless face defeated her. If she'd given herself away it was to no purpose at all; he was the stranger who'd rejected her outside the lifeboat station, with half Hugh Town looking on. She'd been a fool if she'd expected anything else – a stubborn Highlander wasn't a man to change. But with her feet now apparently clamped to the exposed perch of honesty, she could only go on.

"Rupert was very kind to me at a time when I was lonely and unhappy, and I mistook gratitude for love. In Peter's case I couldn't mistake true friendship for anything but what it was – that's why I haven't married him. Nor, to make the record complete, am I in love with Robin Grayson, Michael Harding, the Town Crier or Charley's Aunt. If you look upon Tresco as your personal property I'll stay away from it in future should our visits unluckily coincide again. But now Ulysses and I will continue our walk."

She'd delivered this masterly summing-up without the barest glance at his face – had no way of knowing that it had changed until he finally spoke as if communing with himself.

"She didn't mention *you*, Hugo my boy; now I wonder why that was?"

The sorrowful question trapped her into looking at him, and her much-put-upon heart stumbled, then raced again. He was smiling now, and not only that; all the rueful amusement and tenderness and joy the world could hold seemed to be in his face. When he moved near enough to hold out his hands she put her own into them, knowing the gesture for what it was – acceptance, surrender and the beginning of all contentment.

"Anna, could you climb down off your high horse, please, and listen to me? I came to see you after Judith left because that's where foolish instinct immediately led me. You spurned me – brutally, I have to say – but by the time I knew *why*, I also knew how deeply my friend loved you. Judith had been right about *that*, so it seemed that she was probably right about your feeling for him as well; hence my behaviour at the lifeboat station, when all I really wanted to do was to wrap my arms about you and never let you go." His mouth smiled, but his eyes offered a different message. "It's what I very much want to do now, but there's more to say first. I knew the moment I asked Judith to marry me the mistake I'd made, but I was feeling sick and sorry for myself, and as jealous as hell at seeing you with Neville. I thought if I could at least make *her* happy, something would be salvaged from the wreck. One more mistake, of course – we could never have made it work. I was light-headed with relief when I came to call on you at the cottage."

Anna stared at him gravely, with a confession of her own to make. "I'd had Judith's letter the day before – explaining among other things that you *might* be able to forget her enough to take me on in order to save me from otherwise certain perdition! Let's pray Tangiers makes her happy, or someone else will suffer for getting in her way."

Hugo lifted her hands to his mouth and kissed them, then smiled unsteadily. "I wanted to make love to you here once before . . . want to now, but an upbringing in a Scottish manse marks a man for life, and I'd really rather marry you first! *Will* you marry me, my darling, and be the light and solace of my life?"

She nodded, unable to put her answer into words; then, for fear it wasn't enough, reached up to kiss his mouth. His arms pulled her close, but Ulysses misunderstood a gesture he hadn't seen before and hurled himself at the friend who'd suddenly turned attacker. Caught off balance, Hugo lost his footing, and they ended on the ground in a tangle of arms and legs and helpless laughter. Pleased with what he'd achieved, Ulysses now licked them both impartially, until Anna clambered to her feet, and could implore her dog to behave himself. Then, suddenly serious again, she stared at Hugo.

"Harriet wants to throw a party tonight, and Peter will be there. Can we *not* say anything . . . pretend that we—"

The rest of what she was going to say was interrupted by his hand laid gently across her mouth. "Sweetheart, we could be completely dumb, and still transparent as glass, illuminated by joy. Before this evening you can break the news to Harriet, and I must tell my old friend." His expression was sad for a moment, then he smiled again. "Would Ulysses object, I wonder, if I chastely kissed the tip of your nose before we make for the jetty? That's where my boat is."

That evening she'd just finished her conversation with Harriet when Hugo arrived to escort her to the party. He'd barely kissed her before the telephone rang again, this time with Miss Emily Grayson on the line.

"Anna . . . Mummy says three bridesmaids might

be too many, but *you* don't think so, do you?" she enquired anxiously.

The bride-to-be kept her voice equally serious with a great effort. "I don't see how I could possibly manage with less."

A sigh of relief echoed down the line, but there was another problem to be aired. "If it's going to be soon – springtime – we think white because of my awful red hair . . . with green velvet ribbons, please, and a green bow for Ulysses."

There was the sound of a slight tussle at the other end of the wire from which Harriet emerged the winner.

"Anna, you don't actually have to put up with my daughters at your wedding, in white with green ribbons or anything else."

"You mean I have a choice in the matter?" Anna asked, voice now quivering with amusement.

There was a thoughtful silence while Harriet surveyed the three small faces in front of her. "Well, not much, I suppose . . . Emily's already chosen the pattern for their dresses!"

Anna put down the telephone and collapsed helpless with laughter into Hugo's waiting arms. When she could trust her voice she explained the matter to him. "We shall have to attend, of course, but we needn't expect to be noticed. The girls have got the wedding all arranged."